SIZZLING SIXTEEN

JANET EVANOVICH

LARGE PRINT
Oxford

Copyright © Evanovitch Inc., 2010

First published in Great Britain 2010
by
Headline Review
an imprint of Headline Publishing Group

Published in Large Print 2011 by ISIS Publishing Ltd.,
7 Centremead, Osney Mead, Oxford OX2 0ES
by arrangement with
Headline Publishing Group
an Hachette UK Company

LP

British Library Cataloguing in Publication Data
Evanovich, Janet.
    Sizzling sixteen.
    1. Plum, Stephanie (Fictitious character) - - Fiction.
    2. Bail bond agents - - New Jersey - - Fiction.
    3. Detective and mystery stories.
    4. Large type books.
    I. Title
    813.5'4–dc22

ISBN 978–0–7531–8826–2 (hb)
ISBN 978–0–7531–8827–9 (pb)

Printed and bound in Great Britain by
T. J. International Ltd., Padstow, Cornwall

SIZZLING SIXTEEN

Thanks to Laura A. Koppe
for suggesting the title for this book.

CHAPTER
ONE

My Uncle Pip died and left me his lucky bottle. I suppose I'm fortunate, because he left my Grandma Mazur his false teeth. So I've got this bottle now, and I don't exactly know what to do with it. It's not like I have a mantel. My name is Stephanie Plum, and I live in a bare-bones apartment on the outer edge of Trenton, New Jersey. I share the apartment with my hamster, Rex, and he doesn't know what to do with the bottle, either. The lucky bottle is the size and shape of a beer bottle. The glass is red, and it looks hand blown. It's not entirely ugly, especially if you like beer, but it's also not exotically pretty. And so far, it hasn't been very lucky. I have the bottle sitting on my kitchen counter, between Rex's hamster cage and the brown bear cookie jar that holds my gun. It was Monday morning, halfway through June, and Lula was in my apartment doing a pity pickup because my hunk-of-junk car was dead and I needed a ride to work.

"Hunh," Lula said. "What's that red bottle on your counter?"

"It's my lucky bottle."

"Oh yeah, what's so lucky about it? It don't look too lucky to me. Looks like one of them designer beer bottles, only it's got a fancy glass stopper in it."

"It's my inheritance from Uncle Pip."

"I remember Uncle Pip," Lula said. "He was older than dirt, right? Had a big carbuncle on his forehead. He was the one wandered out of the senior complex a couple weeks ago during that thunderstorm, pissed on a downed electric wire, and electrocuted himself."

"Yep. That was Uncle Pip."

I'm a bond enforcement agent, working for my cousin Vinnie, and Lula is the office file clerk, wheelman, and fashion maven. Lula likes the challenge of fitting her plus-size body into a size 8 poison-green spandex miniskirt and leopard-print top, and somehow it all comes together for Lula. Lula's skin is milk chocolate, her hair this week is fire-engine red, and her attitude is pure Jersey.

I'm a couple inches taller than Lula, and where her body is overly voluptuous, mine is more 34B. My idea of fashion is a girl-cut stretchy T-shirt, jeans, and sneakers. My skin is nowhere near chocolate, my shoulder-length, naturally curly hair is plain ol' brown and often pulled back into a ponytail, my eyes are blue, and I'm still trying to find my attitude.

I hung my purse on my shoulder and pushed Lula to the door. "We need to move. Connie called ten minutes ago, and she sounded frantic."

"What's with that?" Lula said. "Last time Connie was frantic was never."

2

Connie Rosolli is the bail bonds office manager. My heritage is half Italian and half Hungarian. Connie is Italian through and through. Connie is a couple years older than I am, has more hair than I do and a consistently better manicure. Her desk is strategically placed in front of Vinnie's door, the better to slow down stiffed bookies, process servers, hookers with obviously active herpes, and a stream of perverted degenerates with quick-rich schemes hatched while under the influence of who-knows-what.

I live ten minutes from the office on a day without traffic. This wasn't one of those days, and it took Lula twenty minutes to get her red Firebird down Hamilton Avenue. Vinnie's bail bonds business is located on Hamilton, just up from the hospital and between a dry cleaner and a used-book store. There's a front room with large plate-glass windows, an inner office where Vinnie hides, a row of file cabinets, and behind the file cabinets is storage for everything from guns and ammo to George Foreman grills held hostage until some poor burger-loving slob comes up to trial.

Lula parked at the curb, and we pushed through the door into the front room. Lula plunked herself down on the brown fake-leather couch that was positioned against the wall, and I settled into an orange plastic chair in front of Connie's desk. The door to Vinnie's office was open, but there was no Vinnie.

"What's up?" I asked Connie.

"Mickey Gritch snatched Vinnie. Last night, he caught Vinnie in a compromising position, pants down on Stark Street, on the corner of Stark and Thirteenth.

And from what I've pieced together, Gritch and two of his boys dragged Vinnie at gunpoint into the back of a Cadillac Escalade and took off."

"I know that corner," Lula said. "That's Maureen Brown's corner. Maureen and me used to hang out back when I was a 'ho. She wasn't as good a 'ho as me, but she wasn't no skank 'ho, either."

Lula worked Stark Street prior to her job as file clerk. She had a rocky beginning, but she's getting herself together, and I suspect someday she'll be the governor of New Jersey.

"Anyway, I guess Vinnie had a run of bad luck at the track, and now he owes Mickey $786,000," Connie said.

"Whoa," Lula said. "That's a lot of money."

"Some of it's interest," Connie told her. "The interest might be negotiable."

Mickey Gritch has been Vinnie's bookie for as long as I can remember, and this isn't the first time Vinnie's owed money, but I don't recall him ever owing this much.

"Mickey Gritch works for Bobby Sunflower now," Lula said. "You don't want to mess with Bobby."

"Is this serious?" I asked Connie.

"Times are tough, and Mickey wants his money," Connie said. "Too many people stiffing him, so they're going to make an example of Vinnie. If Vinnie doesn't come up with the money by the end of the week, they're going to kill him."

"Bobby Sunflower would do it," Lula said. "He made Jimmie Sanches disappear . . . permanently. Lots of other people, too, from what I hear."

4

"Have you gone to the police?" I asked Connie.

"The police aren't my first choice. Vinnie owes this guy for illegal gambling. Knowing Vinnie, it's possible some of the money came out of the business. We used to be owned by Vinnie's father-in-law, you know, but last year we were sold to a venture capital company based in Trenton. The venture capitalists aren't going to tolerate Vinnie's gambling with their money. If this gets out, we could all be out of a job."

"What about the father-in-law?" Lula asked. "Everyone knows he got a lot of money. Plus, he could squeeze Bobby Sunflower."

Vinnie's father-in-law is Harry the Hammer. As long as Vinnie does right by Harry's daughter Lucille, it's all good, but I suspect Harry wouldn't be happy to hear Vinnie got snatched while he was boffing a Stark Street 'ho.

"Gritch already went to Harry. Not only won't Harry fork up the money to spring Vinnie, if Vinnie gets out of this alive, Harry will bludgeon him to death," Connie said.

"Well, that settles it then," Lula said. "I guess it's adios, Vinnie. Personally, I could use one of them breakfast sandwiches from Cluck-in-a-Bucket. Anyone interested in a Cluck-in-a-Bucket run?"

"If there's no Vinnie, there's no bail bonds office," Connie said. "No bail bonds office means we don't get paid. We don't get paid, and there's no Cluck-in-a-Bucket for anyone."

"That's not good," Lula said. "I'm used to a certain standard of living. Cluck-in-a-Bucket is one of my first

5

food choices. Not to mention I got bills. I charged a fabulous pair of Via Spigas last week. I only wore them once, so I guess I could take them back, but then I don't have shoes to wear with my new red dress, and I got a date Friday worked around the dress."

"We don't have a lot of options," Connie said. "We're going to have to do this ourselves."

Vinnie was like a fungus on my family tree. He was a good bail bondsman, but a slimeball in every other aspect of his life. He had the slim, boneless body of a ferret. He wore his brown hair slicked back, his pants too tight, his shoes too pointy, and he left too many of his sleazy shirt buttons unbuttoned. He wore multiple rings, chains, bracelets, and, on occasion, an earring. He gambled on everything, fornicated with anything, and wasn't beyond an adventure into the kinky. But the truth is, in spite of all this, deep down inside I was worried about Vinnie. When times were tough, and no one else would give me a job, Vinnie came through for me. Okay, so I had to blackmail him, but the bottom line is he gave me the job.

"I'd like to help," I said, "but I don't have that kind of money."

That was a gross understatement. I didn't have *any* kind of money. I was a month behind on my rent, my car was trash, and my boyfriend's dog ate my sneaker. Actually, I use the term *boyfriend* loosely. His name is Joe Morelli, and I'm not sure how I'd categorize our relationship. Sometimes we were pretty sure it was love, and other times we suspected it was insanity. He's a Trenton plain clothes cop with a house of his own, a

6

grandmother from hell, a lean, muscled body, and brown eyes that can make my heart skip beats. We grew up together in lots of ways, and the truth is, he's probably more grown up than I am.

"I wasn't thinking of money," Connie said. "You're a bounty hunter. You find people. All you have to do is find Vinnie and bring him in."

"Oh no. No, no, no. Not a good idea. This is Bobby Sunflower we're talking about. He's mean! He wouldn't like it if I stole his hostage."

"Hey, girl," Lula said. "They're gonna ventilate Vinnie if you don't do something. And you know what that would amount to."

"No Via Spigas?"

"You bet your ass."

"I wouldn't know where to begin," I said.

"You could begin with Ranger," Lula said. "He knows everything, and he's got a thing for you."

Ranger is the other man in my life, and if I described my relationship with Morelli as confused, there would be no words for my relationship with Ranger. He's former Special Forces, currently runs and partially owns a security firm, is drop-dead handsome in a dark, Latino kind of way, and is sex walking. He drives expensive black cars, wears only black clothes, and he sleeps naked. I know all this first-hand. I also know prolonged exposure to Ranger is dangerous. Ranger can be addictive, and it's a bad addiction for a traditionally raised woman like me, since his life plan doesn't include marriage. For that matter, considering the number of enemies Ranger's made, his life plan might not even include living.

"Do you have any suggestions other than Ranger?" I asked Lula.

"Sure. I got lots of suggestions. Mickey Gritch is easy to find. Vinnie got him in his Rolodex. Hell, Gritch probably has a web site and a Facebook page."

"Do you know where he lives? Where he conducts business? Where he might have Vinnie stashed?"

"No. I don't know none of those things," Lula said. "Hey, wait a minute, I know one of them. I know where he does business. He does it from his car. He drives a black Mercedes. It's got purple pimp lights running around the license plate. Sometimes I see him parking in the lot next to the 7-Eleven on Marble Street. It's a good spot, since it's close to the government buildings. You work all day in government, and you want to either blow your brains out or buy a lottery ticket."

"What about Bobby Sunflower?" I asked her.

"Nobody knows where he hangs. He's like the Phantom. He comes and goes and disappears like he's smoke."

"I guess we could sit at 7-Eleven and watch for Gritch," I said.

"Hold on," Connie said. "Let me run him through the system. If he owns a car, I can give you a home address."

People have a television idea about bounty hunters chasing felons down back alleys and kicking in doors in the middle of the night. I've chased a few guys down back alleys, but I've never mastered the art of

8

door-kicking. Mostly, real bounty hunters track people on the computer and make sneaky phone calls pretending to be conducting a survey or delivering a pizza. The age of electronic information is pretty amazing. Connie has computer programs that will help you access your next-door neighbor's third grade report card.

"I have a couple addresses for Gritch," Connie said. "One is his home address and the other is his sister's. Her name is Jean. Looks like she's a single mom. Works at the DMV. I have six business properties for Bobby Sunflower. A pawnshop, a garage, a car wash, a residential slum on Stark, a titty bar, and a mortuary."

The translation was that Sunflower was into fencing stolen goods, chopping up stolen cars, laundering money, pimping women, and probably the mortuary had a crematorium.

"So I guess we gotta keep Vinnie from visiting Bobby Sunflower's mortuary," Lula said.

"What about all my open bonds cases?" I asked Connie. "Last week you gave me six guys who failed to appear for court. And that was on top of a stack of older files. I can't look for Vinnie and find felons at the same time."

"Sure we can," Lula said. "Probably half of those idiots you're looking for will be at Sunflower's titty bar. I say we go do some surveillance, and first thing, we stop at the bakery. I changed my mind on the breakfast sandwich. I'm in a doughnut mood now."

I followed Lula out of the office, and three minutes later, we were parked at the curb in front of Tasty Pastry.

"I'm only getting one doughnut," Lula said, getting out of the Firebird. "I'm on a new diet where I only have one of anything. Like I can have one pea. And I can have one piece of asparagus. And I can have one loaf of bread."

We walked into the bakery and conversation stopped while we sucked in the smell of sweet dough and powdered sugar and we gaped at the cases of cakes and pies, cookies, cinnamon rolls, doughnuts, and cream-filled pastries.

"I don't know what I want," Lula said. "How can I choose? There's too much, and I only got one doughnut. I can't be making a mistake on this. This is critical. I could ruin the whole rest of the day if I pick the wrong doughnut."

I had my doughnuts bagged and paid for and Lula was still undecided, so I went outside to wait in the morning sunshine. I was debating which of the two doughnuts I'd eat first, and before I reached a decision, Morelli's green SUV rolled to a stop in front of me.

Morelli got out and walked over. His black hair was curling along his neck and over his ears, not by design but by neglect. He was wearing jeans and running shoes and a blue button-down shirt with the sleeves rolled. At six foot, he was half a head taller than me, which meant if he stood close enough he could look down my tank top.

"Are you working?" I asked him.

10

"Yeah. I'm riding up and down the street doing cop things." He hooked his finger into my scoop neckline and looked in.

"Jeez," I said.

"It's been a while. I wanted to make sure everything was still there."

"You could ask!"

"If I guess what's in the bakery bag, do I get one of the doughnuts?"

"No."

"You got a Boston Cream and a jelly doughnut."

I narrowed my eyes at him. "How do you know that?"

"It's what you always get."

The door to the bakery was shoved open, and Lula barreled out. "Okay," she said. "I'm ready to go rescue Vinnie." She realized Morelli was standing next to me, and she did a fast stop. "Oops."

"Rescue Vinnie?" Morelli asked.

"He's sort of missing," I told him.

Morelli took the Boston Cream out of the bag, ate half, and gave the rest to me. "Word on the street is that a bunch of people are very unhappy with Vinnie. Word is he owes a lot of money. Do you need help?"

"Would I have to file a police report?"

"No, but you'd have to give me the rest of the doughnut."

"Thanks for the offer, but I have some leads. I'll stumble along on my own this morning and see what turns up."

Morelli gave me a quick kiss and jogged back to his car.

I looked at the two bags Lula was holding. "I thought you were getting just one doughnut."

"And that's exactly what I did. I got one of everything. I'm telling you, this is a beauty of a diet."

We sat at the small table in front of the bakery and ate our doughnuts while I read through the files on Mickey Gritch and Bobby Sunflower.

"We have home addresses for Gritch and his sister, but I can't see Gritch stashing Vinnie in either of those places," I said to Lula. "That leaves Bobby Sunflower's businesses. The pawnshop is on Market Street, the car wash is in Hamilton Township, and the rest are on Stark Street. Let's do drive-bys and see if anything jumps out at us."

"Might as well do the car wash first," Lula said. "If I like the looks of it, I might let them wash my Firebird."

CHAPTER
TWO

Bobby Sunflower's car wash was next to Figaroa Diner. It didn't look like it had a lot of room for holding a bail bondsman hostage, but it advertised brushless washing and personal attention, so Lula got into line.

"I don't know about this car wash," I said to Lula. "I don't like the looks of the attendants."

"You mean on account of they're waggin' their tongues at us and making kissey sounds?"

"Yeah." Plus the multiple piercings, tattoos, ridiculous homey pants, and I was pretty sure one of them had a boner.

"They're just bein' boys," Lula said.

I looked in my bag to see if I had pepper spray or a stun gun.

The pack of idiots swaggered over to us, and one leaned in the window at Lula.

"Hey, momma," he said. "We gonna wash your car like it never been washed before."

"This isn't no ordinary car," Lula said. "This is my baby. I don't want to see no scratches on it when you're done."

"You be nice to me and my boys, and we'll wash your baby by hand."

"How nice do I gotta be?" Lula asked.

"Real nice," he said, smiling wide so we could see he had industrial-grade diamonds embedded in his decayed teeth.

"That's disgusting," Lula said. "You need to show some respect and act like professional car washers. And get your head out of my window."

"I think me and my boys need to show you what we got and maybe we teach *you* some respect."

Lula pulled her Glock out of her purse and stuck it in his face.

"You got ten seconds before I blow your nose off," Lula said.

"Yow, momma!" the guy said.

They all turned and ran, and Lula squeezed off six rounds, managing to miss all of the car washers at pretty much point-blank range.

"Hunh," Lula said, rolling her window up and driving out of the lot. "They don't make these guns like they used to. I can't believe I didn't hit a single one of those fools."

Next stop was the pawnshop. Lula parked on the street, and we got out and looked around. There was an apartment above the shop, but so far as we knew, it wasn't owned by Sunflower. A consignment store was to one side of the pawnshop and a pizza place was to the other side.

"This doesn't look promising," I said to Lula, "but I'm going to go in and scope it out."

"Who am I?" Lula wanted to know. "Am I good cop or bad cop?"

"You're nothing. There's no cop. We're just browsing and leaving."

"No problemo. I can do that. I'm a excellent browser."

We went inside the pawnshop, Lula walked up to the counter, looked in the display case, and called the pawnshop guy over.

"It's not like I need the money or anything, but I was wondering how much I could get for this ring I got on," Lula said. "As you could see, it's got a ruby in the middle with some diamond chips around the edge. And it's in a genuine gold setting."

"Is that a real stone?" he asked her.

"You bet your ass it's real. A gentleman gave me this ring for certain favors. He bought it for his wife but decided I earned it."

"I don't suppose you have any documentation. Like an appraisal."

"Say what?"

"I guess I could give you forty-five."

"Forty-five hundred?" Lula asked.

"No, just forty-five. Cripes, lady, what do I look like, a sap?"

"No, you look kinda hot," Lula said, leaning her boobs on the counter. "What have you got in that back room, sugar?"

"There's no back room. Just a bathroom that even *I* won't use."

"Movin' on," Lula said. And she turned on her heel and sashayed out of the pawnshop.

Ten minutes later, we were idling in front of Sunflower's garage on lower Stark. It was a one-story cinder-block structure with three bays, all doors open.

"I can't see them keeping Vinnie here," I said to Lula. "There are too many people around, and there's no space to hide someone."

Next stop was the topless bar. The neon sign was flashing, and electronic dance music dribbled out the open door. A wasted guy in a baggy white T-shirt leaned against the graffiti-covered building, smoking. He looked at us through slitted eyes, and Lula drove on.

"Nothing but trouble there," she said.

We parked in front of the mortuary and stared at the building. Brown brick, two stories. Upper windows were blacked out. There was a magenta-and-black awning over the door, and MELON FUNERAL PARLOR was written on the awning.

"I don't know what's more depressing," Lula said, "this dreary-ass funeral home or a titty bar in the morning."

"Maybe the bar was serving breakfast."

"I didn't think of that," Lula said. "I guess that would be okay."

"This place has real hostage potential. I'd go in and pretend I'm a customer, but I don't look like I belong in this neighborhood."

"You mean on account of you're the only white woman on this whole street, dead or alive?"

"Yeah."

16

"I see your point, but I'm not going in there. I hate funeral parlors, and I hate dead people even more. I get the creepy crawlies just sitting here thinking about it."

"Okay, we'll do this later. Let's take a look at the apartment building."

The apartment building was half a block away and looked like the Tower of Terror. It was four stories tall, black with grime, and slightly lopsided.

"Holy bejeezus," Lula said, eyes bugged out, looking at the building. "This is scaring the crap out of me. This is like where Dracula would live if he didn't have any money and was a crackhead. I bet it's filled with rabid bats and killer snakes and hairy spiders as big as dinner plates."

I thought it looked like it would be filled with despair and craziness and broken plumbing. Either way, it wasn't anywhere I wanted to go. Unfortunately, it was also a good place to stash Vinnie.

"How bad do we want to find Vinnie?" I asked Lula, unable to take my eyes off the hellish building.

"The way I see it, either we find Vinnie, or I'm gonna be working the fry basket at Cluck-in-a-Bucket. Not that there's anything wrong with the fry basket, but all that grease floatin' in the air isn't gonna be good for my hairdo. And what if they already got someone working the fry basket? What if I can't get another job and they come repossess my Via Spigas?"

And what if I don't come through, and they kill Vinnie? How could I live with that? I thought.

I speed-dialed Ranger's cell phone.

Ranger picked up and there was a moment of silence as if he was sensing me at the other end, taking my body temperature and heart rate long distance. "Babe," he finally said.

"Do you know the slum apartment building Bobby Sunflower owns on Stark?"

"Yes. It's on the same block as his funeral home."

"That's the one. I'm going in to look for someone. If you don't hear from me in a half hour, maybe you could send someone to check."

"Is this a smart thing to do?"

"Probably not."

"As long as you know," Ranger said. And he disconnected.

"I got two doughnuts left," Lula said, "and I'm eating them before I go in just in case I don't come out."

I angled out of the Firebird. "Take them with you. If I don't go in now, I'll chicken out."

The front door was ajar, leading to a small, dark foyer spray-painted with a bunch of gang symbols. Stairs going up to the left. A bank of mailboxes to the right. No names on the mailboxes. Most were open and empty. Some didn't have doors at all. The message was clear. If you lived here, you didn't get mail.

Two doors led off the foyer. Lula and I listened at the doors. Nothing. I tried one of the doors. Locked. The second door opened to cellar stairs.

Lula poked her head in the doorway. "There's stairs going down, but I can't see nothing. It's blacker'n night down there. Don't smell too good, either."

"I hear scritching sounds," I said to Lula.

"Yeah, I hear it, too. Kinda squeaky."

And then a tsunami of rats swept up the stairs and over our feet.

"Rats!" Lula yelled. "*Rats!*"

I was frozen to the spot, too horrified to move. Lula was dancing, arms in the air, shrieking. The rats were wall to wall, scrambling around in a pack, filling the foyer.

"Kill 'em. Kick 'em," Lula said. "Help! Police! Call 911."

I snatched the bakery bag out of her hand and pitched a doughnut out the front door. The rats ran after the doughnut, and I slammed the door shut behind them.

Lula collapsed against the wall. "Do I look like I'm having a heart attack? Did I get bit? Do I have fleas?" She took the bag back from me and looked inside. "At least you didn't throw the jelly doughnut. I was saving that one for last."

I closed the cellar door and took to the stairs. There were three doors on the second floor. Two were nailed shut with crisscrossed boards. No sound from inside. The third was open, and the one-room apartment was empty of people and furniture but filled with garbage.

"I'm going home and taking a shower when we're done here," Lula said. "I feel like I got cooties."

The third floor had three doors, and all were closed. "We need a plan," I said to Lula.

"You mean like I be the Girl Scout cookie girl?"

"Yeah."

"What if Vinnie's in there and he's with some of Sunflower's stooges? We shoot them, right?"

"Only if we have to."

Lula took her Glock out of her bag and stuffed it into her pants, snug to her backbone. She looked at me. "Don't you want to get your gun ready to go?"

"I don't have a gun."

"What have you got?"

"Hairspray."

"Is it firm hold? I might need some when we're done here, depending on what we do for lunch."

I crept down a couple stairs and pressed myself against the wall, hairspray at the ready should Lula need backup.

Lula knocked on the first door, the door opened, and a fat, sloppy, bleary-eyed guy answered. He was maybe fifty years old, needed a shave, needed a shower, needed less alcohol.

"Yeah?" he said.

"I'm sellin' Girl Scout cookies," Lula said, looking past the fat guy into his room.

"Aren't you sorta old to be a Girl Scout?"

"Not that it's any of your business, but I'm doing this for my niece," Lula said. "She got a intestinal disturbance and couldn't make her quota, so I'm helping out."

"What's in the bakery bag?"

"That's none of your business, either. Are you gonna buy cookies, or what?"

The guy snatched Lula's doughnut bag, slammed the door closed, and locked it.

20

"Hey!" Lula said. "You give me back my bag." She put her ear to the door. "I hear the bag rustling! He better not be fingering my doughnut." Lula pounded on the door. "Give me my doughnut back or else."

"Too late," he said through the door. "I ate it."

"Oh yeah, well, eat this," Lula said. And she hauled her Glock out and drilled a bunch of rounds into the door.

"Holy crap!" I yelled, rushing at Lula. "Stop shooting. You can't just shoot up someone's door over a doughnut. You could kill the guy."

"Damn," Lula said. "I'm outta bullets." She scrounged around in her purse. "I know a got a extra clip in here somewhere."

The door banged open and the fat guy looked out at us and ratcheted the slide back on a sawed-off shotgun. He took aim, and I blasted him with hairspray.

"Yow!" he hollered, rubbing at his eyes. "Shit, that stings."

Lula and I flew down the stairs. We took one flight, rounded the corner for the second flight, and crashed into two of Ranger's men on their way up. We hit them with enough force to knock them off balance, and we all went ass-over-teakettles, rolling in a pack to the foyer floor.

"Jeez," I said, getting to my feet. "I'm sorry. I didn't expect anyone to be on the stairs."

I knew one of the guys. His name was Hal. He was a real sweetie, and he was built like a stegosaurus.

"Ranger sent us to check on you," Hal said. "We just got here, and we heard shots."

"Some moron ate my jelly doughnut," Lula said. "So I shot him."

Hal cut his eyes to the third floor. "How bad is he? Do you want us to, you know, get rid of anything?"

"Like a body?" I asked.

"Yeah," Hal said.

"Thanks, but not necessary," I told him. "Lula shot through the door, and the moron came after us with a sawed-off."

"Gotcha," Hal said. "I'll pass it on to Ranger."

Hal and his partner got into their shiny black SUV, and Lula and I got into the Firebird, and we all drove off.

"It's too bad we didn't get to check out all the apartments," Lula said, "on account of I had a real feeling about that place. I could see Vinnie getting hid there."

I thought the apartment building was too obvious. I didn't know Bobby Sunflower personally, but from everything I'd heard, he didn't sound like a dope. If Bobby Sunflower was behind this, probably Vinnie wasn't on one of Sunflower's properties. People like Sunflower had their fingers in lots of pies, and that's where I thought Vinnie was being kept . . . in one of Sunflower's pies.

"Now what?" Lula wanted to know.

"Drop me at RangeMan."

CHAPTER
THREE

RangeMan is housed in a discreet seven-story building on a quiet side street in Trenton proper. If you didn't look closely, you wouldn't notice the small brass plaque by the side of the door that simply states RANGEMAN. No other sign identifies the business. Ranger's private lair occupies the top floor. Two more floors are dedicated to employee apartments, and the remainder of the building runs the security operation. RangeMan services private residences and commercial properties for clients who need a high level of protection. Plus, RangeMan does the occasional odd job of guarding bodies, finding bodies, and possibly eliminating bodies.

Ranger was my mentor when I first went to work for my cousin Vinnie. I suppose he's still my mentor, but now he's also my friend, my protector, from time to time he's been my employer, and on one spectacularly memorable occasion, he was my lover. I have an electronic key to the underground garage and to Ranger's private apartment. It also gives me access to the building, but today I let the guy at the first-floor reception desk buzz me in. I took the elevator to the control room and walked past the cubbies and consoles, waving to men I knew.

Ranger's office was a few steps down the hall. He was on the computer when I walked in, and he smiled when he saw me. A big thing for Ranger, since he doesn't do a lot of smiling. He was dressed in RangeMan black T-shirt, cargo pants, and running shoes. Everyone in the building was dressed exactly like this, but Ranger's clothes fit him better. Possibly because Ranger was clearly at the front of the line when God was handing out the good body parts. You could dress Ranger in a black plastic garbage bag, and he'd still look hot.

"I need a tracking lesson," I said to Ranger. "You know how you always know my location? I want to be able to do that. I want to put one of those gizmos on some-one's car."

"I can give you the gizmo," Ranger said. "And I can show you how to install it, but it won't do you any good if you can't receive the signals. It would be easier and less expensive if you let me track this person for you."

"That would be great. I need to know where Mickey Gritch is going. He's kidnapped Vinnie, and I have to get Vinnie back."

"Why?"

I blew out a sigh. "It's the right thing to do."

Ranger opened his desk drawer, took out a set of keys, and tossed them to me. "You need a car."

"So you're giving me one?"

"It's the right thing to do," Ranger said.

RangeMan keeps a fleet of shiny new black cars for employee use. Most are SUVs. There are a couple

24

F150s and a couple vans. And Ranger's personal car is a Porsche Turbo. The car I drew in the RangeMan lottery was a black Jeep Wrangler.

It was noon when I parked the car in front of the office, and Lula and Connie had two pizza boxes open on Connie's desk.

"That's a lot of pizza for someone only eating one of everything," I said to Lula.

"I'm not eating from Connie's box," Lula said. "I got myself one pizza and that's what I'm eating, but if you want a piece, you could help yourself."

Lula's pizza had the works, and Connie had a cheese and pepperoni pizza. Since I was in a cheese and pepperoni mood, I went with Connie's pizza.

"Let me guess where you got the shiny black car," Lula said. "I'm guessing Ranger."

"It's a loaner."

Lula selected another piece. "Do you know what I think? I think that man is all bad and scary silent on the outside and soft and mushy on the inside."

I knew Ranger pretty well and I wasn't sure what was on the inside, but I knew it wasn't soft and mushy.

"Have you heard any more from Mickey Gritch?" I asked Connie.

"No. I got a phone call first thing this morning and nothing since. I guess Mickey called Lucille last night. Lucille called Harry, and Harry made a few inquiries and found out about the hooker. And by the time I talked to Lucille, she was having the locks changed on the house, and Harry was on a rant. I got the clear impression no one on that side of the family cares if Mickey Gritch offs Vinnie."

"That's a shame," I said. "I know Vinnie brought all this on himself, but it's still sad."

I ate two pieces of pizza, chugged a bottle of water, and hiked my bag onto my shoulder.

"Where you going?" Lula wanted to know.

"I have Ranger tracking Mickey Gritch, so I thought I'd take the afternoon to try to find Dirk McCurdle. He's still in violation of his bond."

"I thought his name was McCuddle," Lula said.

"Nickname," I told her.

The papers branded him McCuddle because he married four women before the state of New Jersey wised up and arrested him. Besides being tagged for bigamy, McCurdle got caught shoplifting some very expensive lingerie. He said social security didn't give him enough money for him to keep up with the anniversary presents.

"He looks like a nice little old man in his newspaper pictures," Lula said.

Dirk McCurdle was seventy-two years old, five-foot-nine tall, pleasantly plump and pink-cheeked, had wispy white hair and a face like a cherub.

"I have a feeling McCurdle is with one of his wives," I said. "One is in the Burg, one's on Cherry Street, and two are in Hamilton Township."

"Hold on," Lula said. "I'll go with you in case one of those wives gets out of hand and you need backup."

I glanced at the file Connie had given me. McCurdle's first wife was his age. All the other wives were in their late seventies. Probably, I could handle them.

"Anyway, I never saw any bigamist wives," Lula said. "I want to see what they look like."

I thought I'd start with the most recent wife and work my way back. Margaret McCurdle lived in a garden apartment in Hamilton Township. The buildings in the complex were two-story redbrick with white doors and white shutters at the windows. There were ten apartments in each building. Five up and five down. Margaret lived in an end unit on the ground floor.

"This looks real normal," Lula said, swinging out of my Jeep, taking in the faux colonial columns in the front of the building. "This don't look like a bigamist hideout. I hope I'm not gonna be disappointed. I hate when that happens."

We crossed the lot to the front door and I rang the bell. The woman who answered the door was about five foot nothing. Her hair was pale blond and cut short. Her make-up reminded me of pictures of Japanese geisha. Exaggerated bow mouth painted with glossy bright-red lipstick, white pancake make-up, and pencil-thin black eyebrows. She was wearing a magenta velour warm-up suit and white tennis shoes.

"Are you Margaret McCurdle?" I asked her.

"Yes. You aren't more wives, are you?"

"No."

"Thank goodness," she said. "I can't keep track of them anymore. I don't know how Dirk does it. He has wives coming out of the woodwork."

I gave her my card. "I'm a bond enforcement agent," I told her, "and I'm looking for Dirk."

"Good luck," Margaret said on a sigh. "I've given up looking for him. He went out for ice cream two weeks ago and never came back. And now it turns out I'm wife number four. I read about it in the paper. I suppose I should get a lawyer, but they're so expensive."

"What's it like being married to a bigamist?" Lula asked her.

"It's perfect," she said. "He told me he was still managing his company in Des Moines. So he would show up on Thursday night in time to set the garbage out for Friday pickup. And then he would leave early Sunday. He was very attentive, and he was always a gentleman. And he was excellent in bed."

"No kidding," Lula said. "You and McCuddle have a lot of sex?"

"No, but we talked about it."

"Do you know where he is now?" I asked her.

"Jail?"

"Not yet," I said.

Lula and I said goodbye to Margaret McCurdle, and I drove us a half mile to Ann McCurdle's house on Sycamore Street. Ann lived in a small ranch house in a neighborhood filled with small ranch houses. Her house was pale gray, with blue shutters and a blue door. Her yard was tidy, and it looked like someone had just mulched around her azalea bushes.

"This is fascinating to me," Lula said, "because I'm a student of human nature. That's why I was such a good 'ho. I took an interest in my clients. And now here I am seeing all these bigamist wives living in all these different kinds of houses. Don't you think it's fascinating?"

Actually, it wasn't high on my list of things that fascinated me, but I thought it was nice that Lula was fascinated.

I rang Ann's doorbell with Lula hovering behind me. I rang a second time and the door was answered by a wiry old lady with a paintbrush in her hand. She had gray hair the color and texture of steel wool, her bifocals were crooked on her face, and she was dressed in white orthopedic shoes and a shapeless cotton creation that was somewhere between a dress and a bathrobe.

"Mrs McCurdle?" I asked her.

"Yeah," she said. "Me and everybody else." She craned her neck to look past Lula. "This isn't another one of them television interviews, is it? I'm painting my kitchen, and I don't have my hair fixed."

I introduced myself and gave her my card. "I'm looking for your husband," I told her. "Do you have any idea where he might be?"

She pushed a clump of hair back from her face and left a smudge of lemon yellow paint. "I don't know where he is, and if you find him, I want to know so I can hunt him down and wring his neck. He started painting my kitchen this stupid yellow color three weeks ago and never came back to finish."

"It's gonna be real cheery when you get done," Lula said.

"Cheery, my behind," Ann McCurdle said. "Every time I look at it, my blood pressure goes up. I'm popping pills like they're M&M's."

"So I guess marrying a bigamist didn't work out for you," Lula said.

"It could have been worse. Just when I was getting sick of him, he'd go off on a two-week business trip. That's the secret to keeping the magic in a marriage," she said. "You don't see too much of each other. Men are only interested in one thing anyway. S-E-X. And then after they get it, they go to sleep and snore."

"I noticed that," Lula said.

I thanked Ann McCurdle for her help, and Lula and I went back to the Jeep.

"Maybe bigamists aren't as fascinating as I thought," Lula said, cinching her seat belt. "According to the newspaper, none of these wives knew there were other wives. Now that I'm meeting them, I could see how that could happen."

I motored out of the lot and turned onto Klockner Boulevard. "His first wife lives in the Burg. I thought we'd try her next, since it's on our way back to the office."

The Burg is an odd-shaped chunk of Trenton bordered by Hamilton Avenue, Liberty Street, Chambers Street, and Broad Street. I lived in the Burg for my entire childhood, and my parents still live there. Houses are small, yards are narrow, cars are large, windows are clean. This is a neighborhood of hard-working second-generation Americans. Families are extended and proudly dysfunctional. Although dysfunction in Jersey might be hard to measure.

Tomasina McCurdle lived one block in from Hamilton in a single-family house with brown clapboard siding and brown trim.

"This house looks like a turd," Lula said. "How could someone live in a all-brown house? You'd think you were going into a turd every day. It's just my opinion, but I'd find that depressing. When you had company over, what would you tell them? The directions would be to turn off Hamilton and park in front of the house looks like a turd."

I had to admit, it wasn't the most attractive house I'd ever seen, but turd seemed harsh. Truth is, the bottom half of my parents' house was brown, and okay, if I was being honest, it wasn't such a great-looking house, either.

I knocked at the door and a sturdy woman answered. She was early seventies, short black hair shot with silver, wire-rimmed glasses, dressed in a green pants suit, large pearl earrings, lots of perfume.

"Tomasina McCurdle?" I asked.

"That's me," she said. "And I know who you are, too. You're Edna's granddaughter. The one who burned down the funeral home."

"It wasn't my fault," I told her. "People were shooting at me."

"I suppose you're looking for my foolish husband, the bigamist."

"We sure are," Lula said. "And if you don't mind me asking, what was it like being married to a bigamist?"

"It was like being married to anyone else."

"That's disappointing," Lula said.

Tomasina pressed her lips together. "Tell me about it. I was married to that idiot for fifty-one years, and ten years ago, he decided to just up and marry someone else. And then he goes and marries every floozy that comes along. What the heck was he thinking?"

"Do you know where I might find him?" I asked her.

"I imagine he's with one of his home wreckers."

"Other than home-wreckers, is there any place else he might be staying? A relative's house? A close friend?"

"I can't see him with any relatives. His brother died last year. His parents are dead. Our son lives in Delaware, and he'd tell me if Dirk was with him. Ernie Wilkes is his best friend, but Ernie's wife wouldn't put up with having Dirk in the house."

"You look all dressed up," Lula said. "Are you going out someplace?"

"No. I just got home. I was at Karen Shishler's afternoon viewing at Stiva's." Tomasina turned to me. "Your grandmother is there causing a scene because there's a closed casket. The viewing was over, and she refused to leave until they opened the casket."

"Thanks," I said. "If you see Dirk, please call me."

CHAPTER
FOUR

Three minutes later, we were in front of Stiva's funeral home. It was on its third owner since Stiva, but it was still called Stiva's.

"I guess you're gonna go get your granny," Lula said.

"Yeah. I'll just check to see if she's still here."

"I'm gonna wait in the car if it's okay with you," Lula said. "Not that I'm afraid of dead people or anything, but it gives me the willies."

Stiva's is housed in a big white colonial on Hamilton. The front steps are covered in green outdoor carpet, and they lead to a wide front porch that spans the width of the house. I walked into the large lobby and heard Grandma arguing with the funeral director in slumber room number three.

"How do I know she's in there if you won't open the lid?" Grandma said.

"You have my word of honor," he told her.

Mitchell Shepherd owns the funeral home. He bought it a year ago and probably regrets his decision. People in the Burg take their funeral homes seriously, and since the Burg lacks a movie theater or mall, the funeral home is most often the entertainment of choice. Shepherd is a mostly bald man in his fifties. He has a round face, round body, and his funereal uniform is navy suit, white shirt, navy striped tie.

"Just a peek," Grandma said. "I won't tell no one."

"Can't do it. The family wants the casket closed."

Grandma Mazur came to live with my parents when Grandpa Mazur passed on to wherever it is that bacon-eating, whiskey-drinking, gravy-loving people pass on to. She's five foot five on a good day, has tightly permed gray hair, a body that's mostly slack skin on spindle bones, and an attitude only old ladies can pull off.

"I made an effort to come here today, and what good is it if I can't even see the deceased?" Grandma said. "Next time, I'm going to Morton's Mortuary. They never have closed caskets."

Shepherd looked like he'd pay Grandma to go to Morton's. He glanced my way and almost collapsed with relief.

"Stephanie!" he said. "How nice to see you."

"Well, for goodness sakes," Grandma said. "Look who's here. Did your mother send you after me?"

"No. I heard you were creating a disturbance, and I came on my own."

"Just in time to give me a ride home," Grandma said. "No reason to stay here any longer, since Mr Party Pooper won't open the lid for me."

I escorted Grandma out of the funeral home and she stopped short when she saw the Jeep.

"Isn't this a cute little thing," she said. "This is a pip of a car. I always wanted to ride in one of these. How the heck do I get into it?"

Lula climbed into the back seat and reached a hand down to Grandma. I got my hand under Grandma's behind, and we alley-ooped her into the passenger seat.

"Good thing you came when you did," Grandma said. "By the time I walked home, I'd be late for dinner, and we're having pot roast tonight. It wouldn't be right to be late for pot roast."

"I love pot roast," Lula said. "I bet you're having mashed potatoes and gravy with it, too. I *love* mashed potatoes and pot roast gravy."

"You should stay for dinner," Grandma said. "We always got extra."

"If you're sure it's no trouble," Lula said. "I wouldn't want to impose. And I won't eat much on account of I'm on this new diet where I only eat one thing. Like, I only eat one piece of pot roast and one glob of mashed potatoes and one green bean."

"Have you lost weight?" Grandma asked.

"Not yet, but I only just started. I'm still getting the hang of it. Like, what happens when you eat salad? Does it mean you eat one salad? Or does it mean you eat one piece of lettuce and one piece of tomato? It don't matter a lot, since I don't understand the whole salad obsession anyway. Lettuce don't look like a food to me. And if you're gonna eat a tomato, I say put it on a burger."

My parents live in a two-family house. They share a common wall with Mrs Markowitz, and both halves of the house are identical in construction. Living room, dining room, kitchen downstairs. Three small bedrooms and one bath upstairs. Mrs Markowitz has lived next door to my parents for as long as I can remember. Her husband died years ago, and she lives alone now, making coffee cake and watching television. She's painted her half of the house lime green. My parents have always had their house brown on the bottom half and mustard yellow on the top. I don't know why. I expect it's a Trenton thing.

The house hasn't changed much over the years. A new appliance when needed. New curtains. Mostly, it's overcrowded with comfortable nondescript furniture, cooking smells, and good memories.

My mom has always been a homemaker. She's a younger, more filled-out version of my grandma Mazur, and I think I'm cut from some of the same cloth. I have their good metabolism, oval-shaped face, and blue eyes.

My dad is retired from the post office, and now he drives a cab part time. I get my unruly hair from his side of the family. And also my perverted cousin Vinnie.

The table was set for three when we walked in. My mom quickly added two more place settings, and in minutes, my father had his head bent over his plate, forking in meat and potatoes, and my mother was at the other end, trying not to stare at Lula's fire-engine red hair and tiny leopard-print top that showed about a quarter of a mile of cleavage.

"Isn't this nice," Grandma said, looking around the table. "I love when we have guests. It's like a party. What were you two doing in the neighborhood?" she asked me. "Were you looking for dangerous criminals?"

"We were looking for Dirk McCurdle," I told her.

"Wasn't that a scandal?" Grandma said. "Imagine having four wives. No one even suspected. He was such a pleasant man. I would see him at the funeral parlor when the Knights of Columbus would have a ceremony."

"Do you have any ideas where he might be hiding?"

"Did you try all his wives?" Grandma asked. "One of them might still have a soft spot for him."

"I have one left."

"If that don't work, you could try Pip's bottle," Grandma said.

My mother blew out a sigh, and my father murmured something that sounded like crazy old bat.

"Is that the red bottle you're talking about?" Lula said. "The one looks like a beer bottle?"

Grandma helped herself to the mashed potatoes. "Pip swore by that bottle. He said it brought him luck."

"How does it work?" Lula wanted to know. "Is it enough to own it? Do you gotta carry it around? Do you have to rub it like a genie bottle?"

"I don't know exactly," Grandma said. "I never saw Pip use it." She looked over at me. "Didn't it come with instructions?"

"No."

"Bummer," Grandma said.

"The bottle is a bunch of horse pucky," my father said. "Pip was a nut. He didn't know enough to come in out of the rain."

"What about when he won $10,000 in the lottery?" Grandma asked. "How do you explain that?"

"Dumb luck," my father said.

"Exactly!" Grandma said. "It was the lucky bottle."

"What about taking a leak in a thunderstorm and electrocuting yourself?" my father said. "Was that lucky?"

"Probably he didn't have the bottle with him," Grandma said.

"What happened to my pot roast?" Lula asked.

"You ate it," Grandma said.

Lula stared down at her plate. She looked in her lap and on the floor. "Are you sure I ate it? I don't remember."

"I saw you," Grandma said. "It was the first thing you ate."

"Do you think eating something counts if you don't remember?" Lula asked.

No one knew what to say. And my father wasn't going to touch it.

Lula looked down at her plate. She had a spoonful of mashed potatoes and a pea. "What's for dessert?" she asked. "It better not be grapes."

Lula and I were back in my Jeep, heading for Stark Street to check out Sunflower's funeral home. It was almost eight o'clock, and the sun was low in the sky. I'd stopped at my apartment to get a sweatshirt, and Lula had insisted we bring the lucky bottle with us.

"Uncle Pip would probably be alive today if he'd taken his bottle with him," Lula said. "If nothing else, he could have pissed in it instead of on that wire."

"Not likely," I said. "I can't get the stopper out. I think it's glued in."

38

"Let me take a look at that bottle. Maybe I can figure it out."

I stopped for a light and pulled the bottle out of my big leather purse.

Lula worked at the stopper, but it wouldn't budge. "You're right," she said. "This sucker's in for good." She shook the bottle close to her ear. "Don't hear anything rattling around in it." She held it up and looked at it in what little light was left. "Can't see anything in it. The glass is too thick."

I think luck is a weird thing. It's hard to tell if you make it or if it just follows you around. And it seems to me it could just as easily be bad luck as good luck. It's not like it's a constant ability, like playing the piano or being able to cook a perfect omelet.

I cruised by the funeral home, and we scoped it out. There were several cars parked at the curb, and a clump of older men dressed in suits and ties stood talking by the open front door. Lights were on inside. Melon's was having a viewing.

I pulled over and parked half a block away. "I'll wait here, and you go look around," I said to Lula.

"Why do you get to wait here?" Lula wanted to know. "I'm the one hates dead people. I should be the one to wait here."

"You can't wait here. You're the friend of the deceased."

"Fine, but I'm not going in alone. You're gonna have to make yourself blend in. Just tart yourself up some, and everyone'll think you're a 'ho come to visit."

I ratted my hair, put on brighter lipstick, took my sweatshirt off, and rolled my T-shirt so I had some skin showing.

"This is the best I can do," I said.

"You're not all that hot," Lula said. "You're never gonna make any money looking like that."

"Sure I would. I'm the girl next door."

"You don't know much," she said. "You gotta have a short skirt to be the girl next door and you put your hair in two ponytails."

"I thought that was the Catholic schoolgirl."

"The Catholic schoolgirl's skirt is plaid and pleated."

I put Pip's bottle back in my bag, hiked my bag up on my shoulder, and swung myself down from the Jeep. We made our way through the clump of men, through the open door, and into the foyer. Several older women stood by a table with a coffee urn and cups. I could see more women and a couple men in an adjoining room. The casket was in that room. So far as I could tell, this was the extent of the public areas.

"Small funeral home," I said to Lula.

"I guess the embalming goes on upstairs, being that the windows are blacked out, and we know Bobby Sunflower likes to keep rats in his cellars," Lula said.

"I want to see what's down the hall to the left. Stand at the front of it, so no one can see me snooping."

The hall wasn't long. It led to a small kitchen, stairs going up, and two doors. I opened one door to stairs going down. I held my breath and listened for a moment. No squeaking. I flipped the light on and whispered hello. No answer. I didn't want to rescue

Vinnie bad enough to creep down the stairs. I closed the cellar door and tried the second door. It opened directly onto an alley and a small paved parking lot. A hearse and a black stretch Lincoln were parked in the lot. I stepped out onto the cement stoop to get a better look at the back of the building, and the door blew closed behind me. I tried the door. Locked. Crap!

The funeral home was in the middle of the block, with no breaks between buildings. I was going to have to walk down the alley and around the corner to get back to Stark. Ordinarily, no big deal, but this wasn't the sort of neighborhood a girl wanted to stroll around in after dark.

I moved to the alley and looked back at the building. Four windows on the second floor. All blacked out and barred, just like the front windows. I called Lula on my cell phone.

"Where the heck are you?" Lula wanted to know.

"I accidentally got locked out. I'm in the alley. Can you let me back in?"

"Negative. Bobby Sunflower just came down the back stairs, and he's standing in the hall talking to some idiot that's got killer written all over him."

"Go ask them if they've got Vinnie upstairs."

"Funny," Lula said. "Why don't you rub your bottle and ask for X-ray eyes?"

"Are you being sarcastic about my lucky bottle?"

"Yeah, and I regret it. It's not a good idea to disrespect a lucky bottle. I'll meet you at the Jeep. Good thing you at least got your hairspray, 'case you meet up with some of the locals."

CHAPTER
FIVE

I power walked down the alley, keeping to the shadows, where I hoped I wouldn't be seen. I scurried around the corner, and by the time I reached Stark Street, my heart rate was at stroke level. I did some deep breathing and tried to calm myself before I got to the car, so I wouldn't have to listen to Lula go on about how I should carry a gun. Okay, probably she was right, but I really hated guns, and I could never remember where I hid the bullets.

Ranger had a remote door entry on the Jeep, so I beeped us in, and Lula and I sat watching the funeral parlor.

"Do you know Bobby Sunflower?" Lula asked me.

"No."

"He's the tall dude just come out."

"Is Sunflower his real name?"

"So far as I know," Lula said.

Bobby Sunflower was a little over six foot tall. He was lean, with a long face and long cornrows that came to his shoulders. He was dressed in a pinstriped suit and a white shirt that was unbuttoned to halfway down his chest. He had a lot of gold chains around his neck, and I could see his diamond ring from where I sat. He had two men with him who looked like dumb muscle. They stood two steps behind while Sunflower talked to a fireplug guy in a bad-fitting black suit.

"That's the funeral director, Melon," Lula said. "I was watching him from inside."

A black Cadillac Escalade with tinted windows rolled to a stop in front of the funeral home. Sunflower turned from Melon and got into the Escalade's back seat. One of the gunners got into the front passenger seat, the other got in next to Sunflower, and the car moved off down the street.

I put the Jeep in gear and followed the Escalade. I kept my distance, staying about a half block behind. They went all the way down Stark, took State Street to Broad, and I lost them on Broad. Too much traffic on Broad. I lost them when I couldn't run a light.

"I got a bad feeling about Bobby Sunflower," Lula said. "Some people just make you scared inside, and he's one of those people."

I turned off Broad and made my way through the Burg to Hamilton and the bonds office. I dropped Lula at her car and headed for home. I was a block from my apartment building when Mickey Gritch passed me going in the opposite direction. Black Mercedes with purple pimp lights flashing around his license plate. Hard to miss. I cut my lights and made a U-turn on Hamilton. I put a car between me and Gritch, and I put my lights back on.

Gritch turned right on Olden, crossed the railroad tracks, and wound around, ending on Stark. He took the alley behind the funeral home, parked behind the limo, and got out. I was around the corner, on the dark side street, watching with my lights off. Gritch got out of his car, walked to the back door, and knocked. The door opened, Gritch walked in, and the door closed.

I checked my rearview mirror and saw that a car had pulled up behind me. My pulse quickened, and I was about to step on the gas when Ranger angled out of the car and walked to the Jeep.

I got out and stood next to him, and my pulse didn't drop back. Ranger at close proximity on a dark and deserted street would make any woman's heart race.

"You scared the bejeezus out of me," I said to him. "I didn't know it was you at first."

"Chet was monitoring the fleet, and he saw you make a U-turn and start tailing Gritch."

"And you were in the neighborhood?"

"No. I grabbed my keys and came out to watch you in action." He did a full body scan on me. "Is this a new look?"

"Lula and I were here earlier, and Lula thought I'd fit in better if I was a 'ho."

Ranger put his hands to my waist and slid them up bare skin to where I had my shirt rolled and tucked into my bra. He loosened my shirt and smoothed it down.

"You looked cold," he said.

I was pretty sure he was referring to the state of my nipples, and because it was Ranger, I was also pretty sure he knew cold had nothing to do with it.

"I saw Bobby Sunflower leave here about forty-five minutes ago. And now Gritch is here," I told him.

Ranger looked at the back of the building. "And you think Vinnie might be here?"

"The windows are blacked out upstairs. Originally, I thought the embalming rooms were up there, but Lula saw Bobby Sunflower come down the stairs." I reached into the Jeep and got my sweatshirt. "I didn't get a chance to check out anything other than the public areas."

Ranger looked at his watch. "Viewing hours are over. The outdoor light was off when we drove by the front of the building. We can hang here for a while and see what goes down."

I zipped my sweatshirt and leaned against the Jeep with Ranger. He wasn't a guy who made a lot of small talk, and I'd gotten used to the silence. We stood like that for about ten minutes, and the door opened and Gritch stepped out. A second guy appeared in the doorway. He flipped the inside light off, and the mortuary parking area was plunged into darkness. We heard the back door click closed, and moments later, car doors opening and slamming shut. Ranger pulled me away from the Jeep, under cover of a building. He leaned into me and shielded me with his body. He was dressed in his usual black. Black T-shirt, black windbreaker, black cargo pants, black running shoes, black gun. His hair was dark brown and his skin was light brown. Ranger was a shadow.

Two car engines turned over, and headlights flashed on. The Mercedes rolled past first. The big Lincoln followed. They took the corner and headed for Stark Street.

Ranger stayed pressed against me, his hand at my waist, his breathing even. His lips brushed my ear, and my cheek, and found my mouth, and the contact produced a rush of heat and desire that filled every part of me. Since we were standing on a public street in a part of town that had killings nightly, I suspected this wasn't going any farther than kissing.

"Are you playing?" I asked him.

"Yes," he said, "but that could change."

I felt my fingers curl into his shirt, and I made an effort to uncurl them. I put a couple inches between us, and I smoothed out the wrinkles I'd made.

"I need to find Vinnie," I said.

Ranger looked over at the building. "Get in your car and lock the doors. I'll go inside and look around."

"I'm sure the funeral parlor has an alarm system."

"Even with the best alarm system, there's a ten to fifteen minute window before anyone responds. And in this part of town, the response is a lot longer . . . if at all."

Ranger jogged to the back door, and within seconds, he had the door unlocked. He slipped inside, and a couple minutes later, I heard the alarm go off. I gripped the wheel and watched the building, keeping track of the time. Five minutes went by. Ten minutes. I had my teeth sunk into my lower lip, and I was thinking *get out, get out, get out!* The door opened at fourteen minutes. Ranger emerged alone and jogged back to the car.

"I'll follow you home," Ranger said. "I don't want to talk here."

46

I pulled away from the curb, and when I got to the corner, the stretch Lincoln slid to a stop in front of the funeral home and three men got out and went to the front door. Ranger and I drove past them and continued on down Stark.

Ranger walked me to my apartment and stepped inside.

"Obviously, Vinnie wasn't being held at Melon's," I said to him.

"The embalming room is in the basement, and it isn't pretty. The upstairs rooms are being used as a cash drop. There's a counting table and a safe in one of the rooms. The other rooms are storerooms. No sign of Vinnie."

"What about Mickey Gritch? Did he make any more stops?"

"I checked with Chet. Mickey Gritch went straight home from Melon's. Looks like he's settled in for the night."

Ranger unzipped my sweatshirt. "We could be settled in for the night, too."

I moved a step back from him. "Are you feeling domestic?"

The corners of his mouth softened into the smallest of smiles. "I'm feeling friendly." He closed the distance between us, lifted my bag off my shoulder, and his focus moved from me to the bag.

"Are you carrying?" he asked. "This bag is heavy."

"It's the bottle."

I took Uncle Pip's bottle out of my bag and set it on the kitchen counter. Rex came out of his soup-can house and looked through the glass aquarium at the bottle. His beady black eyes glistened, his whiskers whirred, and he put two little pink feet on the side of his cage. He blinked once and turned and scurried back into his soup can.

"Why are you carrying this bottle?" Ranger asked.

"This is the bottle I inherited from my Uncle Pip. It's supposed to be lucky, and Lula decided we needed to carry it with us . . . just in case."

Ranger's smile widened. "Can't hurt," he said.

"Well, it didn't do me any good tonight."

"The night isn't over," Ranger said. "You could still get lucky."

Being a bond enforcement agent almost never requires me to set my alarm clock. Felons are in the wind twenty-four hours a day, so I can pretty much pick which of those hours I want to go hunting. Lula usually rolls into the office around nine, and I'm usually right behind her. This morning was no different.

I'd sent Ranger home early the night before, deciding I wasn't ready to get that lucky. A night with Ranger was tempting, but the cost would be high. My relationship with Morelli was currently on hold. A morning argument in Morelli's kitchen a couple weeks ago had ended with the notion it might not be a bad idea if we saw other people, but the reality was that we weren't. I felt comfortable with flirting and maybe a kiss, but I wasn't comfortable going beyond that with another man right now.

"Hey, girl," Lula said from the bonds office couch, "what's up for today?"

"Dirk McCurdle and a drug guy named Chopper."

"And Vinnie," Connie said.

"Yeah," I said. "And Vinnie."

"Do you have any leads?" Connie asked.

"I know where he isn't," I told her. "I'd like an address for Dirk's best friend, Ernie Wilkes. I've got one Mrs McCurdle left. If she isn't helpful, I'll talk to Ernie."

Connie punched a few keys on her computer, and it spit out Ernie's address. She wrote the address on a slip of paper and handed it to me. "He's retired from the button factory, so he should be at home."

The phone rang and Connie picked it up. "Yeah," she said. "Yeah, yeah, yeah. I'll be right there." She disconnected and grabbed her purse. "I have to bond out Jimmie Leonard. That means I have to lock the office up for an hour until I get back."

"We could stay here and babysit phones," Lula said.

"No way," Connie said. "I want you out there looking for Vinnie. I can't be office manager and bond out people at the same time. I know Vinnie's slime, but he pulls his weight here . . . at least some of the time."

Connie and Vinnie were the only ones authorized to write the bonds that released people from jail while they waited for their day in court. I worked as the office bounty hunter, and I signed individual contracts that gave me permission to root out felons who were FTA for their court date. Lula wasn't authorized to do anything, so she just did whatever the heck she wanted.

Connie took off for the courthouse, and Lula and I piled into the Jeep. Stella McCurdle lived in north Trenton. Ernie Wilkes and his wife lived a couple blocks from Stella. Good deal for me. I was short of gas money and not excited about the idea of driving all over creation to find McCuddle. I took Olden to Bright Street and turned onto Cherry. I parked in front of Stella's house, and Lula and I got out and went to the door.

"Now this here's more what I'm talking about," Lula said. "This looks like a bigamist house."

It was a narrow, two-story single-family house. And it was painted lavender with pink trim. Why Lula imagined a bigamist should live in a lavender house was anyone's guess.

"Yep," I said. "This looks like a bigamist house for sure."

"I got high hopes for this wife," Lula said.

Stella McCurdle answered the door in tight lavender stretch pants, little sling-back heels, and a stretchy flower-print wrap shirt that displayed a decent amount of over-tanned, crêpe paper-skinned boob. She had big chunky rings on her fingers and big chunky earrings, lots of make-up, and her hair was a shade short of canary yellow, done up in a seventies bouffant.

"Whoa," Lula said. "It's like *Soul Train* for seniors."

Stella leaned forward. "What was that, dear? My hearing's on the blink. I'm all clogged up with wax. I was just on my way to the doctor."

"I'm looking for your husband," I said to Stella.

"What?"

"Your husband."

"No, thank you," she said. "I don't need any."

"Must be a *lot* of wax," Lula said.

"Dirk!" I yelled. "Where's Dirk?"

"Dirk! Don't know. Don't care," she said. "I'm moving on. I'm gonna find myself a new boy toy. Dirk was too old for me anyway."

"That's the spirit," Lula said.

"What?" Stella yelled. "What did you say?"

Lula and I screamed goodbye to Stella, we got back into the car, and I drove to Ernie's house. I didn't think Dirk was living with Ernie, but I thought Ernie might be talking to him.

"What time is it?" Lula asked. "I might need a doughnut. Is it doughnut time?"

"I'm thinking about eating healthier," I said. "More vegetables and fewer doughnuts."

"What's that about?"

"I don't know. It just came over me."

"It's a bad idea. What do I look like, Mr Green Jeans? How would it sound if I said it's vegetable time? People would think I was a nut. Nobody gets a craving for a vegetable. And I'm on the one diet. What am I gonna do with one carrot or one asparagus? They're not mood enhancers, if you see what I'm saying."

"I see what you're saying, but there aren't any doughnuts between here and Ernie's house."

"I guess I could wait. And maybe you're right about the healthy eating. I'm gonna get a carrot cake doughnut."

I drove a block, pulled over, and called Ernie. I had a feeling he'd be more helpful if I got him away from his wife. My guess was his wife wouldn't be happy to learn he was still palling around with Dirk the bigamist.

Ernie answered and I introduced myself.

"Is your wife home?" I asked him.

"Yes," he said.

"Would she be upset if she knew you were still friends with Dirk McCurdle?"

"What's this about?"

"I can knock on your door and talk to you in front of your wife, or we can meet somewhere for just a couple minutes. I need to find Dirk."

"Okay."

"Just go out in your car or go for a walk, and I'll follow you."

"Okay."

And he hung up.

Five minutes later, a car pulled out of the Wilkeses' driveway and headed for Olden. The car pulled to the curb after three blocks and Ernie Wilkes got out.

"I don't know anything about Dirk McCurdle," Ernie said to Lula and me. "We used to be friends, but I don't see him anymore."

"When was the last time you talked to him?" I asked.

Ernie hesitated a beat. "A long time ago."

"Try again," I told him.

Ernie blew out a sigh. "A couple days ago. He's got a new wife. At least, he says she's a wife."

"Do you know her name? Do you know where she lives?"

"Her name's Dolly. I don't know her last name. He said they met at the Senior Center on Greenwood. And he said she has a house close by there."

"Does Dirk have his own place?"

Ernie shook his head. "Not that I know about. He's always lived in his wives' houses. I tell you, he's a real character."

I thanked Ernie, gave him my card, and Lula and I took Olden to Greenwood.

"Hold up here," Lula said. "There's a bakery on the right, and I bet they've got healthy doughnuts. Like maybe they got a whole wheat and green bean cruller."

CHAPTER
SIX

I pulled into the small lot and waited while Lula ran in. I had my window down, and I was in a zone, staring into the bakery, not thinking. My skin prickled at the nape of my neck and a rush of heat fluttered through my stomach. I caught a hint of Bulgari Green shower gel and knew the reason for the heat. Ranger.

He bent to talk to me through the open window. "There's a problem in the Atlanta office," he said. "I'm on my way to the airport. I should be back sometime tomorrow. In the meantime, call Tank if you need help. I've asked Chet to report Gritch's travels directly to you."

Tank was Ranger's next in command. He was the guy who watched Ranger's back. His name said it all.

"Thanks," I said. "Be careful."

Ranger smiled at that. Hard to tell if he was smiling because someone cared enough to say be careful, or if he thought the idea was funny.

Minutes after Ranger left, Lula hauled herself up into the Jeep. "The best I could do was blueberry," Lula said. "They didn't have no vegetable doughnuts. And I got a strawberry jelly-filled, and a pumpkin spice, and a banana scone. Wait a minute. Is pumpkin a vegetable? Does that count?"

"You must have eight hundred calories in that bag."

"Yeah, but the diet says I can have one of anything."

"One doughnut! Not one of each kind."

"You don't know that for sure," Lula said.

"Have you lost any weight on this diet?"

"No. I gained a couple, but I think it's water retention."

The Senior Center is in a big old house that was remodeled to accommodate bingo. It runs night and day and it smells like crackers. I've learned from past experience that it's best to park on the far perimeter of the lot. At least half the seniors who come for pinochle or bingo are legally blind from macular degeneration, and they park by feeling their way along with their bumpers.

I left Lula in the Jeep with the doughnuts, and I crossed the lot and went straight to the admin office just inside the Center's front door. An older woman in a turquoise smock was at the desk. She looked up at me and smiled.

"Yes, dear," she said. "How can I help you?"

"I'm looking for my grandmother's friend, Dolly."

"You must mean Dolly Molinski. She isn't here right now. In fact, I haven't seen her for some time."

"Do you know where she lives? Do you have a phone number?"

"No, I'm afraid not. We don't keep any of that information. I know she lives close, because she would walk to bingo when the weather was nice."

I returned to the Jeep and called Connie. "Dolly Molinski," I said. "Can you get me an address?"

A couple minutes later, Connie came back on the line. "She's on Stanley Street. Number 401 Stanley."

"I don't know Stanley," I said to her. "I'm at the Senior Center. Can you give me directions?"

"She's two blocks away. Take Applegate to Stanley."

I drove two blocks down Applegate, turned at Stanley, and parked in front of 401. It was a tidy little white house with a postage-stamp front lawn presided over by a three-foot-tall ceramic gnome. Lula and I marched up to the front door, and I knocked. The door opened and a lady not much taller than the gnome looked out at me. She had short snow-white hair, a pleasant round face, and she was wearing shocking-pink yoga pants and a matching short-sleeved T-shirt.

"Yes?" she asked.

"I'm looking for Dirk McCurdle," I told her. "Is he here?"

"Yes," she said, "but he's sleeping. Honestly, I don't know how that man can sleep like he does. I've already gone to my tai chi class, put a stew in the slow cooker, and fed the cats."

"It's important that I talk to him. Could you wake him?"

"I can try, but he's a very sound sleeper."

She sped off, and Lula and I stepped into the living room. It was filled with overstuffed furniture and cats.

56

There was an orange cat on the couch, a striped cat next to the orange cat, a black cat draped over a chair back, and a second tabby cat sprawled on the floor.

"There's cats everywhere in here," Lula said. "And I'm allergic to cats. I'm gonna have a cat attack."

Dolly hustled back into the room. "He's still sleeping," she said. "Maybe you can come back some other day."

"Dirk!" I yelled. "Bond enforcement. I need to talk to you."

Nothing.

"Are you sure he's here?" I asked Dolly.

"Of course he's here. It's Tuesday. I don't mean to be rude, but I'm real busy. I'm behind schedule. I've got kitty litters to clean, I gotta get the car in for service, and I'm meeting the girls for lunch."

"Do you mind if I take a look for myself?" I asked her.

"No. Go right ahead. I'd get him up for you, but I haven't got the time. He's a wonderful man. He can play bingo with the best of them, but he's slow as molasses in the morning. Bedroom's in the back."

I moved past Dolly to the back of the house and the master bedroom, pushing cats out of my way as I walked. I could see Lula from the corner of my eye, shooing cats away, holding her nose.

Lula and I inched into the room and looked at Dirk.

"Uh-oh," Lula said.

I bit into my lower lip. "How long has Dirk been sleeping like this?" I yelled to Dolly.

"Since last night. He went to bed early. Said he had indigestion."

I hauled my cell phone out of my bag and called 911. "We need an officer at 401 Stanley Street," I said. "And an EMT truck, hold the siren."

"Is there something wrong?" Dolly asked.

"I'm really sorry, but I'm pretty sure Dirk's dead," I told her.

Dolly took a close look at him and poked him. "Yep, he's dead all right. Damn. This is the third husband that's died on me in the past year. I've got to start marrying younger men. Good thing I didn't take his name. The red tape is awful." She smoothed a wisp of hair down on McCurdle's head. "He was fun," she said. "I'll miss him on Mondays and Tuesdays."

Lula sneezed. "Damn cats. I gotta get out of here. I'm allergic to just about everything in this house . . . cats and dead people, and pretty soon it's gonna be filled with cops."

Dolly looked at her watch. "I should probably cancel my service appointment."

"You might want to do that," Lula said. "But if we hurry things along, you could make lunch."

"We should go out and wait for the police," Dolly said. "They can never find this house. I don't know why. It's the house with the gnome, for goodness sakes."

"Guess you're getting good at this," Lula said.

"The husband before Dirk died five months ago, he should rest in peace. And before that was George."

58

We all meandered out of the house and stood blinking in the late morning sun.

A cop car angled to a stop behind my Jeep and Carl Costanza and Big Dog got out. Carl and I did Communion together, and he was friends with Morelli.

Carl looked at me and smiled. "I bet this is going to be good," he said.

"I have a dead FTA in there," I told him.

"Did you kill him?"

"No. Looks to me like natural causes, but what do I know. Dolly said he just never woke up."

Carl pulled on rubber gloves.

"Gonna need more than that in there," Lula said. "There's cats." And she sneezed and farted. "S'cuse me," she said.

An EMT truck turned the corner and Big Dog flagged it down.

"I'll stop at the station later today for my paperwork," I said to Carl.

"Don't rush. I have to get mine done first."

"I'm sorry for your loss," I said to Dolly.

"Thank you," she said. "It was nice meeting you."

Lula and I got into the Jeep, and I found my way back to Greenwood.

"That was a downer," I said to Lula.

"Yeah," she said. "It was anticlimactic after waiting all this time to see the bigamist."

"I can't figure out if I'm more depressed that Dirk died or that Dolly didn't know he was dead."

"I take a philosophical view on these things, since I'm a observer of human nature," Lula said. "I figure

59

you gotta have the right attitude about this stuff. Take Dolly, for instance. Dolly was gonna try to keep her lunch date, which is a good thing, because life gotta go on. And even though he was dead, Dirk sort of looked like he was smiling."

"He did look like he died smiling."

"See, it's all part of the circle of life," Lula said. "And pretty soon, we'll be dead, too, only you'll go first because you're older than me."

"Do you have any doughnuts left? I need a doughnut."

"I ate them all, but we can stop at the bakery again. They had some red velvet cupcakes that I'm pretty sure were made with beet juice. Either that or red dye #13."

I hooked a left into the bakery lot and bought myself a doughnut with white icing and colorful sprinkles. "This is a happy doughnut," I said to Lula.

"Fuckin' A," Lula said. "But then I never saw a sad doughnut."

I ate my doughnut and felt much better, so I drove down Greenwood to Hamilton, past the office, and on to the government buildings on the river. It was lunchtime, and I was guessing Mickey Gritch would be hanging out, looking to run some numbers.

"Oh boy," Lula said when I pulled into the 7-Eleven lot on Marble Street. "You're not gonna do what I think you're gonna do, are you?"

"I'm going to talk to Mickey Gritch."

I spotted his car, parked to the side of the lot. No other cars around it. It was early. Lunch hours hadn't kicked in yet. I pulled up beside him, and his tinted window rolled down.

Mickey Gritch had white-blond hair cut in a sixties Beatle mop style. He had little pig eyes that were always behind shades, a big pasty potato head, and a body gone soft. He was in his late forties, and he was living proof that anyone could be successful at crime in Trenton if he truly worked at it.

"What?" Mickey Gritch asked me.

"I want to talk to you about Vinnie."

"What about him?"

"No one wants to fork up the money."

"Doesn't surprise me," Gritch said. "He's a turd. Don't get me wrong. I like Vinnie. We've done business for a lot of years. But he's still a turd."

"Maybe we can make a deal?"

"Like what?"

"Like you don't kill him, and he can get some kind of a payment plan."

"Listen, if it was me, that would be okay. But it's not me. I don't have anything to do with it anymore. This is Bobby Sunflower's deal, and it's more complicated than you know."

"Complicated how?"

"Just complicated. I don't know. I don't want to know. There's bad people involved. Badder than Bobby Sunflower." He leaned out a little. "Is that Lula? Hey, momma."

"Don't you hey momma me," Lula said. "I'll be out of a job if they off Vinnie, and then what? I got bills to pay. I got a standard of living."

"I got a job for you," Gritch said.

"Hunh," Lula said. "I don't do that no more, you little runt-ass Polish sausage."

The tinted window rolled up on Gritch's Mercedes. I put the Jeep in gear and drove out of the lot.

CHAPTER
SEVEN

"Things are going good today," Lula said. "We haven't been shot at or nothin'. Have you got the bottle with you?"

"No. I left it at home."

"Imagine if you had the bottle."

"I've got Chopper's file in my bag," I said to Lula. "Pull it out and read me his address. I think he's off South Broad."

"I'm not sure I want to go after someone named Chopper," Lula said. "Suppose he got his name chopping off fingers and toes. I don't want to lose none of mine. I couldn't wear peep-toe shoes. It would limit my fashion potential."

"Does it say anything in his file about fingers or toes?"

Lula paged through the file. "No. His real name is Mortimer Gonzolez, but it says everyone calls him Chopper. And it says he got a pet named Mr Jingles, and you want to be careful about Mr Jingles. I hope it's not a cat. It sounds like a cat name. Just thinking about it makes my eyes itch."

"Has he got priors?"

"Yeah, lots of them. All like this. All for dealin' drugs. Don't see no assault with a deadly weapon in here. Looks to me like he's a businessman. Middle management."

"Did Connie include a map?"

"Yeah. You have to turn right off Broad onto Cotter Street."

I drove down Broad, and I thought about Mickey Gritch. He said he was out of it. I hoped he wasn't so out of it that he couldn't lead me to Vinnie. And what the heck did he mean when he said it was complicated and there were bad people involved? I thought this was about a simple gambling debt.

"Hey!" Lula said. "You just drove past the street."

I hooked a U-turn and doubled back to Cotter. "I was thinking about the conversation with Gritch. How bad would you have to be to be worse than Bobby Sunflower?"

"I hear you," Lula said. "I think Vinnie got himself into a real mess this time."

I drove one block down Cotter, and Lula counted off numbers.

"Here," she said. "He's living over this plumbing supply warehouse. Must be a loft apartment."

Cotter Street was an odd mix of light industrial and residential. Low-income single-family houses were mixed between auto body shops, small warehouse facilities, and a variety of building supply businesses. I drove around the block to see if it was intersected by an alley. Turned out it was, so I drove down the alley and idled behind the plumbing supply warehouse, looking up at the second-floor loft.

"How do you want to do this?" Lula asked. "Girl Scout cookies? Pizza delivery? Census survey?"

There were stairs leading up to a small deck and a back door. So far as I could tell, this was the only entrance. "I'm in a mood to just go up and kick the door down," I said to Lula.

"Me, too. That was gonna be my next suggestion." Lula looked over at me. "You learn how to kick a door down?"

"No. I thought you'd do it."

"I'm wearing four-inch slut shoes. I can't kick a door down in slut shoes. It isn't done. You need boots to kick a door down. Everyone knows that."

"Then I guess we'll ring the doorbell and identify ourselves."

"Whatever," Lula said.

I parked behind a rusted-out Econoline van, and Lula and I got out and walked up the stairs to the deck. There was no doorbell, so I knocked on the door. No answer. I knocked again. Still no answer. I pulled my phone out and dialed Chopper's number. We could hear the phone ringing inside, but no one was answering that, either.

"Too bad we don't know how to break the door down," Lula said. "He might be hiding under the bed."

I stood on tiptoes and felt over the doorjamb and found a key.

"If I was in this neighborhood, and I had a bunch of drug money and drugs stashed here, I'd be more careful about my key," Lula said.

"Maybe he has an alarm system."

I plugged the key into the door, held my breath, and pushed the door open. No alarm sounded. I looked around for an alarm keypad. None visible.

"Guess he's just one of those trusting people," Lula said. "Sort of refreshing in this day and age. Especially in the criminal element."

We were standing in a large room that had a bare-bones galley kitchen at one end, a kitchen table and four chairs, and beyond that a couch and two easy chairs in front of a large flat-screen TV. There was a door to the right, which I assumed led to the bedroom.

"It's just amazin' how normal a criminal could be," Lula said. "This looks just like any other person's apartment. 'Course you gotta sell drugs to afford something this big, but aside from that, you gotta admit it's real normal." She looked around. "I don't see Mr Jingles. And I don't think it's a cat, because I'm not sneezing. I bet it's a cute puppy or something."

"I don't see any dog bowls or dog toys."

"Here, Mr Jingles," Lula called. "Here, boy! Here, Mr Jingles. Come to Lula."

There was a rustling sound behind the couch, and a six-foot alligator padded out, focused on Lula, and lunged.

"Yow!" Lula said, stumbling back, knocking into me. "Help! Watch out. Get outta my way!"

I was across the room like a shot with Lula on my heels, pushing me through the door, slamming the door behind us.

"I think I wet myself," Lula said. "Do I look like I wet myself?"

I was beyond noticing if she wet herself. I had my hand over my heart, and my mouth open sucking air, and my heart was knocking around so hard in my chest my vision was blurred.

"I think we're done here," I said to Lula.

"Fuckin' A," Lula said. "Don't forget to put the key back, or Chopper won't be able to get in to feed Mr Jingles if he locks himself out."

I returned the key to its hiding place, and the gator slammed against the door on the inside of Chopper's apartment and Lula and I flew down the stairs, missing a couple, both of us sliding halfway on our asses. We got to our feet, the gator banged against the door again, and Lula and I ran screaming for the Jeep.

Ten minutes later, I parked behind Lula's Firebird in front of the bonds office.

"I guess that's why Chopper doesn't need an alarm system," I said, finally finding my voice.

"What kind of man keeps a alligator in his house? That's just wrong. Where does he poop? You ever think of that? And he got a lot of nerve naming him something cute like Mr Jingles. That's a deceptive name. And it was all your fault anyway, because you left your bottle home."

My phone rang, and I picked it up to Morelli.

"I need to talk to you," Morelli said. "I caught the McCuddle fiasco. I'm sure the autopsy will show natural causes, but I need you to fill out some paperwork. If you meet me at Pino's in ten minutes, I'll buy you lunch."

"Deal."

"What was that about?" Lula asked.

"Lunch with Morelli. He got assigned to McCuddle, and he's got my paperwork."

Pino's serves Italian food Burg-style. Greasy pizza you have to fold to eat, meatball subs, sausage sandwiches, spaghetti with red sauce, worthless uninteresting salad with iceberg lettuce and pale tomatoes, Bud on tap, and red table wine. It has a dark, carved, mahogany bar and a side room with tables for families and couples who don't want to watch hockey on the television hanging over the liquor collection.

Morelli was waiting for me at a table, choosing not to be distracted by ESPN recaps on the bar television. He had a Coke in front of him and a breadbasket.

I ordered a chicken Parmesan sandwich and a Coke, and Morelli ordered a sausage sandwich. When the waitress left, Morelli handed me a stack of papers.

"I don't need these in a rush," he said, "but I know you have to hand them in to get your capture fee."

I shoved the papers into my messenger bag. "It was a shock to find McCurdle dead like that."

"Yeah, but he actually looked kind of happy."

"He liked being married."

Morelli smiled. "He liked being married too much."

"I have a hypothetical question for you. If Bobby Sunflower was mixed up with someone more scary than him, who would it be?"

"A couple people come to mind. Can you be more specific?"

"Suppose Vinnie was also mixed up in it."

"That doesn't narrow it down a lot. Vinnie was into a lot of illegal stuff. Prostitution, gambling, recreational drugs. In his defense, I have to say to my knowledge he always only bought and never sold."

"Let's narrow it down to gambling."

"That's tough. I'd think Sunflower kept that to himself." Morelli picked a breadstick out of the basket. "I'm guessing this isn't all that hypothetical. Do you want to tell me about it?"

"You'd have police issues."

Morelli leaned back in his chair and locked eyes with me. Serious. "If you were in danger, I'd expect you to tell me."

"I'm okay. Aside from an alligator encounter this morning, everything's under control."

"Were you at the zoo?"

"Cotter Street."

"I imagine you're talking about Chopper's alligator. How big is he now?"

"Has to be six foot."

"I've never seen him, but I've heard stories."

I buttered a piece of bread. "He's prehistoric. Scared the bejeezus out of me. He came out from behind Chopper's couch and snapped at Lula. Lula and I took off and fell halfway down the stairs, and then screamed

69

all the way to the car. Now that I think about it, it was sort of embarrassing."

"Did you apprehend Chopper?"

"No. He wasn't home."

"But he left his door open and unlocked?"

"Something like that," I said.

Morelli looked around for the waitress. "Maybe I should have ordered a drink."

"Feeling the need for alcohol?"

"Yeah, you have that effect on me. My biggest fear is that someday I'm going to show up to arrest someone and it's going to be you."

"Would you do that?"

Morelli gave up on the waitress and slouched down a little. "I'd put the cuffs on you."

"And then what?" I asked.

His mouth curved into a small smile, and his eyes darkened. "Do you want to know the details?"

My turn to smile. "Not here."

"You're teasing me," Morelli said. "I like it."

That led to a long silence while we both considered the next move. It would be easy to fall back into an intimate relationship with Morelli. He was fun, and sexy, and easy to live with. And I liked his dog. He could also be difficult to live with. He hated my job. And he insisted on controlling the television remote. We had a history of breaking up and eventually getting back together. I suppose it suited our current lifestyle, but it was probably establishing bad habits.

"Do you remember why we broke up?" Morelli asked.

70

"You needed space."

"I needed toast. You ate the last piece of bread, and you didn't get more."

"I was busy. I forgot."

"You're supposed to remember those things. You're a woman."

"I'm supposed to remember toast?"

"Yes."

"What about you? What are you supposed to remember?"

"Condoms."

Here's the scary part. It sort of made sense.

"So what's new with you, other than McCurdle?" I asked. "Any interesting murders?"

"McCurdle's about as good as it gets. After him, it's same ol', same ol'. Gang executions, vehicular homicide, accidental death with a blunt instrument."

The waitress brought our sandwiches, and we dug in.

"What can you tell me about Chopper?" I said to Morelli.

"He's middle-management drugs. He used to do enforcement for Ari Santini. If you fell behind on your protection payments, Chopper would shorten your finger. That's how he got his name. One day, he shortened the wrong finger and got his hand smashed with a baseball bat. Had a hard time getting a good grip on finger-chopping tools after that, so he got bumped over to sales."

Oh great. Lula was right.

"Any ideas on how I can catch Chopper?" I asked Morelli.

"I'd avoid his apartment."

A glob of red sauce slipped out of my sandwich and landed on my T-shirt. "Crap," I said, looking down at the sauce.

Morelli's eyes darkened a little, and for a moment I thought he was going to lick the sauce off. And then I wasn't sure if it was because he wanted the sauce or because it was on my breast.

"I already figured out the apartment avoidance," I said, dabbing at my shirt with my napkin. "What else?"

"I don't know. He's not in my circle of friends." Morelli tapped a number into his phone and asked about Chopper. He got off the phone, wrote a bunch of addresses on a napkin, and gave me the napkin.

"Midmorning, he'll be downtown," Morelli said. "He moves around, but he's usually on lower Stark. Drives a black Lexus. He has a lunch trade going at a couple fast-food places around the arena. Then he goes home to stash money and package up more stuff. He's somewhere around the food court at Quakerbridge Mall early in the evening, and then he moves to a multiplex parking lot. Usually in Hamilton Township."

"He covers a lot of ground."

"Yeah," Morelli said. "He hustles."

"And the alligator protects the drugs and the money?"

"Looks that way."

"Two questions. If you guys know where he sells drugs, why don't you arrest him?"

"We did. He's out on bail. And it's not that easy. He's sneaky."

"Okay, second question. Why doesn't someone walk into his apartment and shoot the alligator and take the drugs and the money?"

Morelli stopped eating and looked at me. "You aren't thinking of doing that, are you?"

"Of course not. It was a hypothetical question. Honestly, do you really think I'd shoot an alligator?"

"No," Morelli said. "But Lula might."

"Lula couldn't hit an alligator if it was three feet from her and already dead. I shoot with my eyes closed, and I'm a better shot than Lula."

Morelli's phone buzzed and he looked at the readout. "I have to go," he said.

"Something bad happen?"

"I'm a homicide detective. If they're paging me, it's never good." He stood and dropped a couple twenties on the table. "That should cover it," he said. "Call me if you get lonely."

"What kind of an invitation is that?" I asked.

"I was going for friendly without being pushy."

I shoved back from the table and stood with him. "You succeeded."

CHAPTER
EIGHT

I stopped home to change my shirt, and at the last moment, I decided to take my bottle. I mean, it couldn't hurt to carry it around, right? I left my apartment, and I drove past the bonds office toward the arena. I cruised the area around the arena, looking for Chopper's Lexus, checking out the fast-food places Morelli's source had listed. I hung there until two o'clock without seeing a single black Lexus SUV. I took Broad to Cotter and drove the alley behind Chopper's loft. The black SUV was parked in Chopper's small backyard. Chopper was at home with Mr Jingles.

I returned to Broad, and I was almost at Hamilton when Chet called.

"Gritch left the 7-Eleven and drove across the river. I have him at an isolated house a half mile off Lower Buck's Road. He's been there for ten minutes now. I'm programming it into your nav system."

"Thanks. I'll check it out."

"Do you need backup?"

"Do I have a choice?"

There was a long pause. "No," Chet finally said.

It used to bother me that Ranger monitored my every move, but I've gotten used to it, and for the most part, I'm able to ignore it. Truth is, I'm not all that good at being a bounty hunter, and Ranger's overprotectiveness has saved my life more than once.

I stopped at the bonds office to get Lula, and I ran into Walter Moon Man Dunphy coming out of the used-book store next to the bonds office. Mooner is my age, but he lives on an entirely different planet. He's slim, with light brown shoulder-length hair, parted in the middle. He was wearing a vintage Metallica T-shirt, jeans with holes in the knees, and black-and-white Chucks.

"Dudette," Mooner said to me. "Long time no see. How's life?"

"It's good," I told him. "What's new with you?"

"I got a new casa. It's el loco mobile casa."

It took me a moment to realize he was talking about the rusted-out motor home at curbside.

"You're living in this RV?"

"Affirmative. Totally cool, right? And the feng shui is excellent. Like, if I'm getting bad vibes, I just park this sweetheart in a different direction. And I have a dish, so I didn't have to give up my position on the Cosmic Alliance."

I had no clue what he meant by the Cosmic Alliance, and I didn't want to take the time to ask.

"That's great," I said. "I have to go to work now."

"Yeah, me, too."

"You're working?"

"Gotta feed the Love Bus. Doesn't run on air, dude."

"What are you doing?"

"I'm walking dogs. I pick 'em up, and take 'em to the park, they crap their brains out, and I take 'em home."

He gave me his card. GOLDEN AURA DOG SERVICE. Happy Is As Happy Does.

"Nice," I said.

"I'm hella entrepreneurial," Mooner said. "It's a gift."

I pocketed the card and went into the bonds office. "Gritch is at a house in Bucks County," I said to Lula. "I'm going to take a look. Want to come with me?"

"Sure," Lula said. "Haven't got anything better to do."

"How about filing," Connie said.

"Filing isn't better," Lula said. "Filing gives me a cramp in my head. Personally, I think you should just throw all those files away. We never look at them. What good are they? When was the last time you looked at one of them files?"

"I'd look at them if I could find them," Connie said. She turned to me. "Speaking of files, I got a new one for you. Lenny Pickeral. It should be an easy capture."

"Wait until you hear this," Lula said. "This is a beauty. This guy stole toilet paper outta all the rest stops on the Turnpike. He said he was protesting the inferior quality of rest stop toilet paper."

It didn't seem like such a horrible crime. "They arrested him for that?"

"Actually, they arrested him for making an illegal U-turn across the grass median," Connie said. "When they checked out his trunk, they found it was full of toilet paper. And then they went to his house, and *it* was full of toilet paper. The guy has been stealing toilet paper from the Turnpike for almost a year."

"And now he's FTA?" I asked.

"Probably stealing more toilet paper even as we speak," Lula said. "Sounds to me like a addiction."

I rammed the file into my bag. "Adiós. I'm off to find Vinnie."

"Me, too," Lula said. "I'm gonna find the heck out of him."

I crossed the Delaware River into Pennsylvania and went north on Lower Buck's Road, watching my nav screen. Lower Buck's Road is a two-lane, fairly well-traveled road that runs along the river. It's a mix of expensive homes, moderate homes, and woods. Not a lot of commercial property.

Ten minutes down Lower Buck's Road, I was told to turn left, onto a dirt road. It was a wooded area, and the dirt road was single-lane. I knew the house was a half mile in. I crept along, not wanting to raise dust, and after a half mile, I came to the house. It was a brown-shingle, two-story, cottage-type house. Big. Maybe seven thousand square feet. A Bucks County manor house. Professional landscaping. Circular drive court. Not shabby. Probably, Vinnie didn't want to be rescued. He probably had a Jacuzzi and a four-poster bed. On the other hand, they were going to kill him on Friday.

I continued on down the road, past two more houses, before the road abruptly ended. I turned and slowly cruised past the brown-shingle house for a second time. Gritch's Mercedes was parked in the drive court, plus two other cars. One was an SUV and the other a Ferrari.

"Hard to believe you'd want to stash a perv like Vinnie in a nice house like this," Lula said. "Maybe this here's Bobby Sunflower's house. In which case, we be sitting in Bobby's driveway, and that might not be healthy."

"Good point."

I drove back to the road, pulled to the side, and parked. A half hour later, Mickey Gritch turned out of the dirt road and headed south, toward Trenton. The Ferrari followed.

I called Chet, gave him the Ferrari's plate number, and asked him to find owners for the car and the house. He called me back in five minutes.

"The car belongs to Bobby Sunflower," Chet said. "The house is owned by a holding company. And Sunflower owns the holding company."

"Can you find out if the holding company owns other properties?"

"Sure. I'll get back to you."

"This is like having your own private detective agency," Lula said. "Does Ranger keep a tally of services? Do you gotta pay up one way or another at the end of the month? I tell you, I wouldn't mind doing that. He is heartstoppin' hot. I had my way, I'd spread sauce on him and work him like a rib."

The thought of working Ranger like a rib gave me a hot flash that prickled from my scalp clear down to my doodah.

"You just turned red," Lula said. "I never seen you turn red like that before."

"It was the rib thing."

"Yeah," Lula said. "I get like that about ribs, too. I think we need to go to Tony's when we get back to town. He makes kick-ass ribs."

We sat there for ten minutes more, waiting for the SUV, but the SUV didn't drive by.

"I'm going to leave the car here and walk back to the house," I told Lula.

"I'll come with you. Good thing I dressed down to sneakers today."

I checked Lula out. She was wearing pink wedge sneakers loaded up with rhinestones, a super-short stretch denim skirt, and a way-too-small pink T-shirt decorated with silver glitter that was flaking off on everything. It was casual Tuesday. I was in my usual outfit of jeans, sneakers, and a slightly stretchy V-neck T-shirt. No glitter. No red sauce stains.

"Here's the plan," I said, starting out on the dirt road. "If we hear a car coming, we jump off the road and hide in the woods."

"Sure, I can do that," Lula said. "Only I hope we don't have to, 'cause I have vegetation issues. I don't do the nature thing. Remember when we were down in the Pine Barrens? I hated that shit. I'm a city girl. I like cement. As far as I'm concerned, you could cement this whole country over."

"Maybe you want to stay in the Jeep," I said.

"That might be a good idea. I could stay and make sure it don't get stolen."

The road was hard-packed dirt and either side was forested. The sun filtered through the leaf canopy and the air smelled like the beginning of summer. I would have enjoyed the walk if only I hadn't been terrified Bobby Sunflower would return and run me down.

I moved from the road to the woods just before I got within sight of the house. I'm not as bad as Lula when it comes to nature, but I'm not a tree nymph, either. I've seen Ranger move through brush and never make a sound. As hard as I try to be quiet, I'm more of a thrasher. I crept along the edge of the property, looking for movement inside the house. The SUV was still parked just past the door. Shades hadn't been drawn. There was no way of knowing who belonged to the SUV. No way of knowing if Vinnie was here. I returned to the Jeep and pulled myself up behind the wheel.

"Well?" Lula wanted to know.

"I have no clue. I couldn't see anything in the house. And no one came out."

"Are you carrying the bottle?"

"Yes."

"Hunh, you'd think the bottle would do something for you."

I turned the key and put the Jeep into gear. "I didn't get caught."

"That's true," Lula said. "So it could be working."

It was after four o'clock when we got back to the bonds office. Connie was painting her nails and looking not happy.

"So?" I said.

"I got a call from Bobby Sunflower at two o'clock. He said he was getting impatient. And then he put Vinnie on, and Vinnie begged me to get the money, and then someone started shrieking. I guess that was Vinnie. And the line went dead."

"Bobby Sunflower was at the Pennsylvania house at two o'clock," Lula said to me. "Now we know where they got Vinnie."

"His car was at the house," I said. "We never actually saw Bobby Sunflower."

"That man isn't gonna let nobody drive his Ferrari," Lula said. "That's a personal Ferrari."

Probably true.

"They got Vinnie at this house in Pennsylvania," Lula said to Connie. "We know exactly where it is. We just gotta rescue him now. My Visa bill is due any day. I can't take no chances."

Here was the deal. While I was looking for Vinnie, this sounded like a noble idea. Now that we might have found him and had to go in guns blazing, I was thinking . . . not so good. Morelli could pull this off, but I couldn't ask him without agreeing to police involvement. Ranger would have Vinnie out in a heartbeat, but Ranger was in Atlanta. And even if Ranger were here, it wouldn't feel right to make him do my dirty work.

"Maybe instead of rescuing Vinnie, we should try to raise the money," I said.

"Okay," Connie said. "How?"

We all thought about it.

"We could have a bake sale," Lula said.

"You can't bake, Stephanie can't bake, and I don't want to bake," Connie said. "And we need $786,000. That's a lot of cake. Plus, the interest grows on that every day."

"Now that I think about it," Lula said, "if I had that kind of money, I wouldn't need this job."

"The bonds office is now owned by a venture capital group called The Wellington Company. Last I looked, they weren't happy with the office performance. I don't think we want to rock that boat by asking them for a loan."

"Let's just rescue him and get it over with," Lula said. "How hard could it be? There was one SUV sitting in the driveway. So I'm thinking there's Vinnie tied to a chair in the kitchen and some goon in the living room watching TV."

"And?" I asked.

"And we go in, shoot the goon, rescue Vinnie, and we go home."

"I'm not comfortable with shooting the goon," I told her. "And we aren't a hundred percent sure Vinnie is in the house."

"I know," Connie said. "Stink bomb. We lob a stink bomb in there, everyone runs out, and in the confusion we rescue Vinnie."

"I like it," Lula said to Connie. "Boy, you're good. I could see you've done this before."

"High school," Connie said. "I was the stink bomb queen. One time, I stink-bombed the principal's house and he blamed it on Jimmy Rubinowski."

82

"What happened to Jimmy Rubinowski?" Lula wanted to know.

"Nothing. He was a football player. He was golden."

"Is this stink bomb going to damage the house?" I asked.

"No," Connie said. "It takes a couple days for the smell to go away, but then everything's good. Except for the window you broke getting the bomb into the house."

"I hate to be a wet blanket, but I don't like doing this without making sure Vinnie's in the house," I said.

Lula and I broke a few minor laws from time to time in the pursuit of felons, but for the most part, we had paperwork giving us wide authority for search and capture. We all knew Bobby Sunflower was pond scum, but that didn't give me the right to lob a stink bomb through his window.

"This isn't a whim," Lula said. "There's circumstantial evidence. And anyway, this here's Bobby Sunflower we're talking about. He probably gets stink-bombed all the time."

"How about this," Connie said. "I go home and whip up a stink bomb. And then we go back to the house at night so we can creep around better and look in windows. And then if it looks like Vinnie's in the house, we bazooka the bomb in."

"I guess that's okay," I said. "Unless Sunflower has family in the house."

"Sunflower hasn't got family," Lula said. "Only thing he'd have in the house is armed entourage and maybe a 'ho or two."

"The sun goes down around eight-thirty," Connie said. "So let's meet here at the office at eight-fifteen. And everyone wear black."

"Black's not my best color," Lula said.

CHAPTER
NINE

I left the bonds office, drove to Quakerbridge Mall, and went straight to the food court. I had a photo of Chopper, and I'd become pretty good at spotting drug dealers. Not to mention I had the lucky bottle. So maybe with all those things going for me, I could snag Chopper. I got a cheeseburger and a vanilla shake, and I sat at a table that would allow me to see almost the entire food court area.

According to the photo and file description, Chopper was a Hispanic male, 5'9" tall, medium build, no piercings or tattoos. A smashed right hand. Forty-five years old. One eyebrow.

I finished my burger and shake, and I sat for a while, trying to look like I was waiting for someone. I got up and walked around a little. I bought a chocolate chip cookie. I sat at a different table. I did another tour of the food court. I walked beyond the food court and looked around. No Chopper. I bought an ice-cream cone, and I sat and ate it. Still no Chopper. By seven o'clock I'd had enough of the food court, so I went home and changed into black commando gear. Black jeans, black T-shirt, black sweatshirt.

Lula and Connie were already at the office when I pulled in. Connie was dressed just like me. Lula looked like an ad for S&M clothes for plus-size women. Black leather boots up to her thighs, black stretch skirt that hung two inches below her ass, black Spandex wrap shirt.

"I got my gun, my stun gun, my pepper spray, my flashlight," Lula said. "And then I got my other gun and a bread knife."

"I have an Uzi and the stink bombs," Connie said.

They looked at me.

I had hairspray and a nail file, but it didn't stack up next to guns and stink bombs. "I have the lucky bottle," I told them.

"Now you're talking," Lula said.

Connie grabbed her purse, and we followed her out of the office.

"I've got my brother Tony's car," Connie said. "It's a POS Explorer, and no one will pay any attention to it sitting on the side of the road."

Lula got in front with Connie, and I got in back with the box of stink bombs. The adapted for stink bombs rocket launcher was behind me. It was deep dusk when we drove over the bridge to Pennsylvania, and by the time we reached the dirt road, it was black as pitch out. No moon. Overcast sky. Connie pulled off to the shoulder and parked on Lower Buck's Road just before our turn-off. We all piled out and waited while Connie loaded the rocket launcher up with a stink bomb.

"It's a big house," Lula said. "How many of these bombs do you think we gotta fire off?"

86

"One will probably do it," Connie said, slinging the Uzi strap over her shoulder. "But we could do an upstairs and a downstairs if we want to be sure of covering the whole house."

"What's it smell like?"

"The one I made today smells like a combination of cat pee and diarrhea fart," Connie said, handing me the box with the extra bombs. "And maybe it has a hint of throw-up."

We walked about twenty feet down the road and had no idea where we were.

"I don't know if I'm in the middle of the road or the middle of the forest," Lula said. "I can't see nothin'. There's no light here. There's . . . whoops!"

"Are you okay?" I asked.

"No, I'm not okay. I'm on my ass, and I found the edge of the road on account of I'm in a bush. Where the heck are you?"

"Everyone stay still until our eyes adjust," I said.

"How long's that take?" Lula wanted to know.

"A couple minutes, I think," I told her.

"It's been a couple minutes," Lula said, "and I'm not adjusted. I think that adjusting is a lot of hooey."

"Give it a minute more," I said.

We waited a minute more, but we still couldn't see.

"I'll show you adjusting," Lula said. And she flipped her flashlight on.

So much for the stealth approach.

We followed Lula and her flashlight until we reached the grassy area around the house. Once we were out from under trees, we were at least able to differentiate structure from sky. Light blazed from several windows. A television flickered in a downstairs room. A figure moved from one room to the next. The SUV was still parked by the door.

"We need to get closer," Connie said. "Someone should run across the lawn and look in the windows."

"Someone?" I asked.

"Yeah," Connie said. "You."

"Why me?"

"It's your job. I'm the office person, and you're the sneaking around, chasing down bad guys person."

"What about Lula? Why can't Lula be the sneaking around person?"

"Yeah," Lula said, "what about me? I could sneak your ass off."

"So let me get this straight," Connie said to Lula. "You're the one wants to get thrown under the bus."

"Since you put it that way, it occurs to me Stephanie has the skill sets needed for this operation," Lula said.

I did an eye roll that no one could see, because it was too friggin' dark. I set the box of stink bombs on the ground, laid my purse on it, and I jogged across the lawn to the house. I pushed my way into some big azalea bushes and stood on tiptoe to look in the window. A fifty-something guy was sitting on the couch watching television. He was in his socks, kicked back, with a bag of chips and a beer on the coffee table in front of him. A second guy was slouched in a La-Z-Boy type chair.

I struggled to get out of the azaleas, and I moved around the house, peeking in windows, listening for

88

conversation. I got to the kitchen, and there was a tray on the kitchen counter with some dirty dishes and a can of Coke tipped on its side. There were also a couple dishes, some silverware, and two glasses on the counter by the sink. It could be that someone was served on a tray and two people ate in the kitchen. Not conclusive proof Vinnie was being held in the house, but it was worth considering.

I jogged back to the woods and told Connie and Lula what I'd found.

"I say we rocket a bomb in there and see what comes out," Lula said.

"Suppose only the guys watching television come out?" I said. "Is someone going in to make sure Vinnie isn't there?"

"That would be you again," Lula said, "since you're so good at finding people."

"No." I shook my head. "No, no, no. I already did my thing. Someone else's turn. I'm not going into a house that smells like cat pee and diarrhea fart."

"I'd be happy to do it, but I got asthma," Lula said. "I might have an attack in there. It could kill me."

We were standing at the edge of the woods arguing, and headlights appeared on the dirt road. The car was traveling at a good speed, coming in from Lower Buck's Road, almost on top of us before we saw it. We dove for cover, flat on our stomachs, hidden in shadow. The car roared into the circular driveway, stopped in front of the brown-shingle house, and *Bang* — fired off an object that broke the foyer window. *Bang* — another shot fired at an upstairs window, and the car spun its wheels and careened out of the driveway, back toward the road. It was a dark-colored SUV. I couldn't see the plate or the make. We got to our feet and stood in shock for a moment.

"What the heck was that about?" Lula wanted to know.

In a moment, we knew what it was about, because the inside of the house was engulfed in flames, and smoke billowed out the broken foyer window.

"Firebomb," Connie said.

We ran to the house to make sure everyone got out, and just as we reached the house, three men ran from the opposite side, jumped into the SUV, and took off. Hard to tell in the dark if one of them was Vinnie, it all happened so fast. There was a small explosion from somewhere inside, windows blew out, and flames shot out the windows and licked up the side of the house.

"We need to get out of here," Connie said. "We need to get to the car before the police and the fire trucks show up. The police will wonder why a car's parked there."

I grabbed my purse and the box of stink bombs, and we hustled down the road, with Lula in the lead holding her flashlight.

"Boy, Bobby Sunflower is a really unpopular person," Lula said. "You gotta get in line to bomb his house."

We were walking fast. I was sweating holding the box of stink bombs, and I could hear Lula breathing hard in front of me. We were almost to Lower Buck's Road when we heard the sirens.

"Crap," Connie said. "How did they get here so fast?"

I hiked my bag farther up on my shoulder. "I'm sure the house had a security system, and fire always goes directly to police and the fire department."

A police car was the first on the scene. It turned onto the dirt road, and we jumped into the woods. A second car was close behind, but it stopped on Lower Buck's Road, behind Connie's SUV.

"I'm screwed," Connie said.

The cop sat in his car for what seemed like an eternity. Finally, the driver's door opened, and the cop got out and walked to Connie's car. A beam of light swept over the SUV. We held our breath and didn't move. A fire truck chugged past and turned onto the dirt road. It was followed by an EMT truck. The cop returned to his car, pulled onto the road, and turned into the dirt road.

Connie called the Trenton police and reported her brother's car stolen.

"I parked it at Quakerbridge Mall," she said. "And I just came out of Macy's, and it's not here."

She gave all the necessary information and said she had a ride coming and needed to get home.

"That was quick thinking," Lula said. "It wouldn't be good if Bobby Sunflower found out we were parked here. He'd think we were the fire bombers. The police probably would think that, too."

"Unfortunately, we can't use the car to get home," Connie said. "We're going to have to leave it here."

"I bet your brother's gonna be pissed," Lula said.

Connie shrugged. "He'll understand."

Connie's family took crime in their stride. It was a family activity.

"So how we gonna get home?" Lula wanted to know. "It's getting late, and I got television shows I want to watch."

"My brother Tony would pick us up but his car's on the side of the road," Connie said.

"I got no one," Lula said. "I don't got a special someone in my life right now."

I shoved my hand into my pocket and came up with Mooner's card.

The RV creaked to a stop behind Connie's SUV and Mooner leaned out the driver's side window. "Have no fear, Mooner's here," he said.

"What the heck is this?" Lula said, taking in the hand-painted peace signs, swirly wind, and stars symbols on the side of the bus.

"It's a motor home," Mooner said. "It's a quality recreational vehicle."

Connie sniffed the air drifting out the open window. "It smells like dog."

"Yep," Mooner said. "And it comes by it honest."

We scrambled inside and looked for a place to sit. The walls were covered in velvet-like leopard-print fabric. The couches and chairs were upholstered in fuzzy faux zebra. The tabletop and kitchen counter were red Formica. Even in the dark of night, it was a migraine.

"This here's real nice," Lula said. "Surprisingly plush. 'Course, I'm a animal-print person, myself, so I appreciate the decor."

"I did it myself," Mooner said. "I was going for retro animal kingdom." Mooner ground the RV into gear, performed a U-turn at the dirt road, and headed back to Trenton. "Were you ladies attending the bonfire?" he asked. "It has to be mega. I could see the glow from the bridge."

"We didn't go to the bonfire," I told him. "We were just riding around and the car broke down."

"I could turn this bus around and take you to the fire if you want," Mooner said.

"Not necessary," I told him. "You've seen one fire, you've seen them all."

"So true," Mooner said. "Personally, I'm more a wind man. Wind rocks."

Mooner dropped Connie off at her brother's house, so she could retrieve her car, and he took Lula and me back to the bonds office. Lula got into her Firebird and drove away, and I walked back to the Jeep, where Morelli was waiting for me. He was lounging against the Jeep, arms crossed over his chest.

"Hey," I said. "What's up?"

"You were asking about Bobby Sunflower, so I thought you'd want to know one of his properties burned to the ground tonight."

"Which one burned?"

"His Pennyslvania house."

"Was anyone in the house?"

"It's too early to tell. No one was rescued." Morelli wrapped me in his arms and nuzzled my hair. "You smell smoky," he said.

"Must be from Mooner's motor home. He took us for a demo ride."

"It's not nice to lie," Morelli said.

Our eyes locked.

"Do you honestly want the truth?" I asked him.

Morelli thought about it for a beat. "No," he said.

I stood on tiptoes and kissed him on the nose. "It's late. I have to go home. I have a big day of bounty huntering tomorrow."

His arms were still locked around me. "I could go home with you."

"You'd go home with someone who might be a liar?"

"Yeah," Morelli said. "I'm getting desperate."

"You were the one who wanted to break up. You said I wasn't relationship material."

"I didn't say that."

"You did!"

"Can I take it back? I hadn't had my coffee yet. And I needed . . ."

I narrowed my eyes at him. "You needed what?"

"Toast," Morelli said. He blew out a sigh. "This isn't going to happen tonight, is it?"

"No."

I was getting mad all over again. No one pushed my buttons like Morelli. I mean, why was I the one who had to remember to buy the bread? Okay, in all honesty, I thought this was a pretty stupid thing to break up over. And in all honesty, I should have remembered to buy bread. That didn't alter the fact that I was mad. Mad wasn't a reasonable emotion. And the truth was, I wasn't entirely sure if I was mad at Morelli or mad at myself.

CHAPTER
TEN

I rolled into the bonds office at nine o'clock. Connie was at her desk. Lula hadn't as yet arrived.

"Have you heard anything about the fire?" I asked Connie.

"So far, no bodies found. Word on the street is there's a war going on between Bobby Sunflower and some under-the-radar Mob guy."

"Did your brother get his car back?"

"He's picking it up from impound today. The police suspect it was stolen by someone associated with the fire."

"Only tangentially."

"That's a big word," Connie said.

"I heard it on television. I'm pretty sure I used it right."

The phone rang, and Connie answered. "Yeah," she said to the caller. "I understand." She hung up and looked at me. "That was a reminder that we have two days left to come up with the money. And it's now grown to a million one."

"At least we know Vinnie didn't burn up in the house."

"Looks that way. I suppose it's a good thing, although I'm starting to think it might be easier just to look for a new job."

Lula bustled in. "What'd I miss? Did I miss anything? I overslept. And then I couldn't figure out what to wear. And my coffeepot's broke, so I had to stop at Starbucks, and the line was out the door."

"We found out Vinnie didn't burn up in the house," I told her.

"Hunh," Lula said. "But then on the bright side, since he isn't dead, we might get to use the stink bomb after all."

"Every cloud has a silver lining," Connie said.

"You got bags under your eyes," Lula said to me. "You spend the night with Morelli?"

"No. We're in the off-again phase of our on-again, off-again relationship," I told her. "It was just one of those sleepless nights."

I had bags under my eyes because I'd thrashed around all night in a state over bread. And then I was in a state because I had two men in my life, and I had no clue what to do with them. I loved them each in different ways, and I was too traditional and Catholic to just enjoy them. How sick is that? I wasn't a practicing Catholic, but I had guilt. And I was stuck with all these rules about relationships. And then there was my mother, who I suspect was mortally afraid I'd end up with Ranger. And my grandmother, who probably thought I was an idiot not to be sleeping with both of them. And my father, who didn't think there was a man alive who was worthy of me. So I'd probably gotten about an hour's sleep last night. And then Chet had called at seven o'clock. Midmorning for Ranger's team.

"This morning, Chet called with a list of properties Sunflower owns through his holding company," I told Connie and Lula. "I'm going to do a drive-by on everything that's local."

"I'm up for that," Lula said. "It's a nice sunny day out. Perfect for riding around. Maybe we should put the top down on the Jeep."

For the most part, the holding company owned commercial real estate that was leased out to a variety of businesses. A supermarket, a dry cleaner, a pet store, a hair salon, a natural foods store, and a couple empty lots.

"This is interesting," Lula said. "Here's this Sunflower guy who's real bad, making his money off prostitution and gambling and drugs, and then he's got this whole other side that's got legitimate, boring businesses. Don't you find that interesting? I mean, the man owns a natural foods store."

"He doesn't actually own the store. He owns the physical space."

"Same difference. And a pet store filled with puppies and shit. I mean, can you see Bobby Sunflower selling puppies?"

"He doesn't personally sell puppies."

"But suppose he did. Wouldn't that be weird?"

I'd driven past all the properties on Chet's list and I was now parked on Liberty Street. Nothing on the list had the potential for holding Vinnie captive.

98

"I don't know where to go from here," I said to Lula. "I have two days to find Vinnie, and I'm out of ideas."

"I got ideas," Lula said. "They're about lunch. I'm thinking nachos."

"Good idea," I told her. "I know just the place."

I drove down Liberty to Broad and followed Broad across town to Marble Street. I pulled into the 7-Eleven lot and parked. Mickey Gritch was on the other side of the lot, conducting business as usual.

I gave Lula a twenty. "Get me nachos and a drink. I'm going to talk to Mickey."

"You sure you don't want me behind you doin' backup?"

"No. I can manage on my own."

I waited for a guy in a rumpled suit to walk away from Gritch. When the guy got in his car, I moved in.

"Hey," I said to Gritch. "Long time no see."

"Not long enough," Gritch said. "Get away from me. You're like poison."

"How so?"

"I don't know. By association."

"Talk to me," I said.

Gritch rolled his engine over. "I'm leaving."

"You can talk to me here, or you can talk to me at your house," I said. "I know where you live."

I'd had good luck with Ernie Wilkes with that threat. I figured I'd roll it out and try it again.

"You wouldn't do that," Gritch said.

"Yep," I said. "I would."

"That's not fair. A man's home is his castle."

"Where's Vinnie?"

"I don't know. I swear. I guess he was at Sunflower's house in Pennsylvania, but it got firebombed, and they moved him. I'm serious now. Walk away. Let Sunflower do whatever he has to do to Vinnie. He's dealing with crazy people. I don't even know who they are, but they scare the crap out of me."

"I need a name."

"I don't have a name. I'm not a big player in the organization. I heard Blutto tossed around, but I don't know what it means. I don't know if it's a first name or a last name or a nickname."

"Thanks," I said.

"You're not going to visit me, are you?"

"No."

"Nothing personal, but that's a relief."

I left Gritch to his lunch trade and went back to the Jeep. Lula swung in minutes later with two boxes of nachos and two giant-size sodas.

"What about the one diet?" I asked her. "Aren't you only allowed to have one chip?"

"That diet isn't real specific about meaning one chip or one box of nachos. I'm thinking of quitting that diet anyway. It don't work. I think I'm going to have to look for a new diet."

I finished the nachos, and I was torn between going after Chopper and continuing to look for Vinnie. If I caught Chopper, I might be able to get my car fixed. I loved the Jeep, but it wasn't mine. Eventually, it would have to be returned to Ranger. Especially if I got back together with Morelli. Using one man's car and sleeping in another man's bed didn't work. At least not when the men were Ranger and Morelli. Of course, if I slept with Ranger, I might be able to keep the Jeep indefinitely.

"What the heck are you thinking?" Lula asked me. "You're mumbling and rolling your eyes and sighing."

"I was thinking I need to find Vinnie. He only has two days left."

"Do you think Sunflower would really kill Vinnie?"

"Yes," I said. "I think he'd kill Vinnie."

"I do, too," Lula said. "Sunflower's a bad man."

I finished my soda, collected the trash, and ran it over to the trash can by the door. I ran back and cranked the Jeep over.

"Where we going?" Lula wanted to know. "We've already been all over the place."

"I have a hunch. They had to hustle Vinnie out of the burning house and stash him someplace else. It would have to be someplace easy on short notice. Someplace like an apartment building."

"The rat house."

"Exactly."

In fifteen minutes, we were in front of the apartment building on Stark. The area around the apartment was quiet at this time of the day, but a scrawny guy, who I assumed had a big gun, was slouched on a folding chair by the door.

"That's like an advertisement Vinnie's in there," Lula said.

"Maybe."

I drove around the corner and turned into the alley. We counted off units, and I idled behind the apartment building. It had six parking spaces marked off in its small lot. The rest of the lot was given over to a Dumpster. The black SUV was parked in one of the spaces. The building had a back door at ground level. One window with bars at ground level. No bars on the windows on the second, third, and fourth floors. A rusted fire escape clung precariously to the back of the building.

"Try the back door," I said to Lula.

Lula dropped out of the Jeep, crossed the lot, and tried the door. Locked. She got back into the Jeep.

"Now what?" Lula said. "I think he's in there, but I don't know if the stink bomb's gonna work. This place already smells like a stink bomb. Plus, they got a ticket taker on the front door."

"One of us needs to go in and look around."

"You?"

"No," I said. "You."

"Why me? I'm only the assistant bounty hunter, and I'm not even sure I want to rescue Vinnie."

"You can get by the guy at the door. Tell him you're making a delivery to the nasty fat guy on the third floor."

"Am I goin' door to door, selling Girl Scout cookies?"

"No. Once you get in, just look around and listen for voices."

I dropped Lula off at the corner and watched her swing her ass past the funeral home and up to the guy at the door to the apartment building. She stood and talked to him for a short time, and then she went inside. After ten minutes, I looked in my rearview mirror and spotted a RangeMan SUV double-parked in front of a bar half a block back. The cowardly part of me was happy to see them there, but the rest of my brain acknowledged that I led a weird life. I had a cop boyfriend who hated my job and tried to get me to quit. And I had a security expert potential lover who didn't tell me to quit my job, but had me under constant surveillance. I wasn't sure which was worse.

Lula popped out of the building's open front door, and the door guard grabbed her by the arm. I was ready to roll if it looked like she was in danger. Not that I would be much good as a rescuer, but the two heavily armed, overly muscled guys on my bumper could do some damage.

Lula jollied herself away from the door guard and sashayed down the sidewalk to where I was waiting. She got into the Jeep, I waved to the RangeMan guys, and I drove off.

"Well?" I asked her.

"He's there. He's in the back unit on the fourth floor. I could hear him talking. Sounded like they were playing cards."

"Any problems? Anyone see you?"

"Just the moron at the door, and he bought the 'ho line."

It was too late to catch Chopper at his lunch stops, and I wasn't in the mood to start looking for the toilet paper bandit, so I headed back to the office. I needed to talk to Connie anyway. It was one thing to find Vinnie, it was a whole other deal to rescue him. As much as I would love to see Connie shoot off a stink bomb, I had serious doubts about it as a rescue aid. Seemed to me a stink bomb, like a firebomb, got everyone out of the building, but didn't give us an opportunity to snatch Vinnie.

I was halfway across town when Grandma Mazur called. "I think I broke my foot," she said. "I was dancing to one of them workout videos, and I accidentally stubbed my toe on the coffee table, and now I think something's broke. At first, I thought it wasn't broke, but it's turned purple, and it's all swelled up."

"Where's mom?"

"She's at the beauty parlor. And your father's playing pinochle at his club. And I hate to call the ambulance people, because then I'll be a spectacle. There'll be rumors I'm dead. I just need you to give me a ride to the emergency room."

CHAPTER
ELEVEN

Lula and I stood in the living room, looking at Grandma's foot.

"It looks broke all right," Lula said to Grandma. "That's one heck of an ugly foot you got there, but I like the polish you got on your toes. What's the name of that?"

"Red Hot Rapture. Lucky I just painted them yesterday. Imagine breaking your foot when your toes weren't done up."

"Yeah," Lula said. "I'd hate that. Does it hurt?"

"It used to, but I took a couple snorts of Jack Daniels, and I'm pretty happy."

"We need to get her to the car," I said to Lula.

"Okay," Lula said. "Do you want to carry her or drag her?"

"Can you hop?" I asked Grandma.

"I could before the Jack Daniels, but now I'm not so sure."

Lula got on one side of Grandma, and I got on the other, and we scooped Grandma up and got her out the door, down the sidewalk, and to the Jeep. I was afraid to alley-oop her, so I dragged her up onto the passenger seat.

"It's a shame we gotta go to the hospital," Grandma said. "I feel like having some fun. I wouldn't mind seeing some naked men."

"How much Jack did you have?" Lula asked.

"I don't need Jack to want to see naked men," Grandma said. "You get to be my age, and there's not a whole lot of opportunity. I signed up for one of those porn movies on TV once, and it was all girls. You only got to see the men from the back. What good is that?"

"I hear you," Lula said.

Saint Francis Hospital is about three minutes from my parents' house. I pulled into the emergency room drive-thru, off-loaded Grandma into a wheelchair with Lula in charge, and hustled to the parking garage.

By the time I got back to the emergency room, Grandma had been wheeled off somewhere to be evaluated, and Lula was busy reading magazines.

"This is an excellent emergency room," Lula said. "They got a good selection of magazines. And people tell me they know what they're doing here when it comes to shootings and knifings, on account of they get so much practice."

An hour later, they wheeled Grandma back to the waiting room with a big black boot thing on her foot.

"It's broke, all right," she said. "I got to see the X-ray."

"What have you got on your foot?" Lula wanted to know.

"The bone was just cracked a little, so they wrapped my foot up in this boot thing instead of putting it in a cast. I can walk on it and everything."

106

Grandma got out of the wheelchair and took the boot for a test-drive.

Step, stomp, step, stomp, step, stomp.

The boot came to midcalf, was foam-padded and held secure with thick Velcro straps. The bottom of the boot was two inches of hard molded plastic. When Grandma walked, she was tipped to one side, since one leg was two inches longer now than the other.

"I feel gimpy in this boot," Grandma said. "And my butt cheeks don't match up. One feels higher than the other. I can't squeeze to keep the breezers in."

"We'll keep the windows open on the way home," Lula said.

Grandma looked down at the boot. "It's pretty nifty, though. I can't wait to show this to your mother. I bet this could get us one of those handicap parking signs. And I got some pills for when the Jack Daniels wears off."

I brought the Jeep around to the drive-thru, boosted Grandma up into it, and drove her home. I'd called ahead, and my mother was waiting at curbside.

"Here she is," I said, lowering Grandma down to my mother. "Almost as good as new."

"For the love of Pete," my mother said.

"I was doing a lunge, and I broke my foot," Grandma told her. "But it's only a little bit broke."

"I have to go," I said to my mother. "I have to get back to the office."

"Can you walk?" my mother asked my grandmother.

"Of course I can walk," Grandma said. "Look at this."

Step, stomp, step, stomp, step, stomp.

"Whoops," Grandma said. And she face-planted on the grass.

Lula and I jumped out of the Jeep and rushed over.

"It's the dang boot," Grandma said. "It's got me all lopsided."

Connie was at her desk when we walked into the bonds office.

"We would have been here sooner," Lula said, "but we had to go on a mission of mercy. Grandma Mazur broke her foot dancing to an exercise video, and we had to get her fixed up."

"Is she okay?" Connie asked.

I took my usual seat in front of the desk. "Yes. They put her in an orthopedic boot and sent her home."

"And we got more news," Lula said. "We got good news, and we got bad news, and it's all the same news. We found Vinnie."

Connie's eyebrows rose a couple inches. "Are you serious?"

"They've got him in a back apartment in Sunflower's building on Stark Street," I said. "Lula heard him through the door. They've got a guy in there with him, and there's a guy at the entrance downstairs. There aren't any bars on the back windows, and there's a rusted fire escape, but you'd die trying to get Vinnie out that way."

"Do you have any ideas?" Connie asked me.

108

"No. None. And I don't think the stink bomb will work. They'll haul Vinnie out of the building under armed guard, and they won't let go of him."

"We need a diversion," Lula said. "We need to get the guard out of the apartment. Then someone can go in and drag Vinnie's worthless ass out of there."

"A diversion's a good idea," I said, "but how are we going to get Vinnie down the stairs and out the door past the door guard?"

"We could disguise him," Lula said. "Put him in a wig and a dress or something."

I looked at Connie. "Do you think that'll fly?"

"Maybe if we have a diversion at the front door, too," Connie said.

"I can divert the guy at the front door," Lula said. "He likes me."

"I'll be the second diverter," Connie said. "That leaves Stephanie to get Vinnie out."

"How are you going to divert him enough for me to get Vinnie down the stairs? I don't think a wig's going to do it. And suppose you divert him out of the apartment, but he locks the door behind him? What then?"

"See, that's the problem with you," Lula said. "You're bein' a glass-is-half-empty person. One of my outstanding qualities is my positive personality. You've just gotta take precautions, like you need to bring a gun with bullets in it."

I pulled to the curb in front of the bonds office at precisely nine o'clock. Connie was already there, and

Lula slid to a stop behind me. I was dressed in black. I had a loaded gun pressed against my backbone, stuck into the back of my jeans. I had pepper spray in my pocket. I had my cell phone clipped to my jeans waistband, set to dial RangeMan. I had a stun gun also clipped to my jeans waistband. And I had premonitions of disaster. I had no confidence in the mission. Truth is, we sucked at this stuff. We were like the Three Stooges at Camp Commando. The only reason I was attempting it was because I knew Chet would spot me on Stark Street and send out a backup RangeMan car.

We assembled in front of the office to review the plan. Connie was wearing wedge heels, a short, tight skirt, and a sweater that showed about a quarter mile of cleavage. Ditto Lula, substitute thigh-high hooker boots for the wedge heels.

"I've been thinking about it," I said. "Our best shot at this is to get the back door open." I looked over at Lula. "If you can open the door for Connie and me, we can slip upstairs easier. And then we can bring Vinnie out that way."

"You can count on me," Lula said. "What about cars?"

"We'll take the Jeep," I told her. "I'll drop you off on Stark Street, and then I'll park in the alley behind the building. After we escape with Vinnie, I'll swing around and pick you up."

"Okeydokey," Lula said. "I'll be waiting for you."

We all piled into the Jeep, and by the time we got to Stark Street, my stomach was sick and I had a grapefruit-size lump of panic sitting in the middle of

110

my throat. Lula got out at the corner and walked half a block to the apartment building. There was still a guard out front, but it was a different guy. I circled around and parked in the alley as planned.

"This is going to work, right?" I said to Connie. "We won't get caught, or killed, or anything?"

"Do you have the bottle with you?"

"It's in my purse."

"So that should help," Connie said.

Oh jeez, it was going to come down to the bottle.

Connie got out of the Jeep and adjusted her girls. "Vinnie better appreciate this effort. It's not like I haven't got better things to do than to save his ass," she said.

I reached under my seat and grabbed the two-pound Maglite that was standard equipment on all RangeMan vehicles. It was also the weapon of choice for head-bashing.

There wasn't a lot of light in the alley. There were streetlights in place, but the bulbs had been shot out. We walked to the back of the building and looked up. Shades were drawn on the fourth-floor windows. The black SUV was parked nose-in to the building. I tried the back door. Locked. We both took a step back and waited in the shadows for Lula to unlock the door.

I heard footsteps, the doorknob turned, and Lula looked out at us. "The coast is clear," she said. "The door dummy went down the street to get something to smoke."

"Show time," Connie said. And she motored through the door, down the short hall, and wasted no time going up the stairs.

I followed close behind, thinking I'd done equally dangerous and stupid things as a bounty hunter, but this was right up there with primo bone-head operations. We reached the fourth floor and looked around. Three doors — 4A, 4B, and nothing on the third door. I listened at the unnumbered door. Silence. I carefully tried the knob. Unlocked. Utility closet.

I stepped into the closet and pulled the door almost entirely closed. I heard Connie rap on a door. Heard the door open. Muffled words. Connie was handing the guy a line about her girlfriend passed out on the second floor.

"And she's naked," Connie said. "And we've both had too many cosmos, and I think we're in the wrong building."

I heard the apartment door click closed and then footsteps on the stairs. I slipped out and went to 4B. The door was unlocked. I stepped inside and scanned the room. It was an efficiency with a small kitchenette on one side. Grease-stained pizza boxes on the counter. A card table and a folding chair. An ashtray overflowing with cigarettes. No couch. No television. No wonder Connie had an easy time with the guy who answered her knock. He had to be going nuts in here. I heard something rustle in the other room, and I was hoping it was Vinnie, because the last time I heard something rustle like that it turned out to be an alligator.

I poked my head in and spotted Vinnie handcuffed to a thick chain that stretched into the bathroom.

"Holy shit," Vinnie said. "What the fuck?"

Vinnie was wearing pointy-toed, shiny black shoes, black socks, and black bikini briefs. Vinnie fully dressed wasn't all that good. Vinnie in black socks and briefs was a nightmare.

"Where are your clothes?" I asked him.

"I haven't got any. This is what I was wearing when they snatched me."

There was a moment where I actually debated leaving him there.

"I know what you're thinking," Vinnie said. "And Grandma Plum and Aunt Mim would be very upset if you left me here and they killed me."

"Okay," I said, "but how am I supposed to rescue you when you're chained to the toilet?"

"You don't have a universal key? What kind of bounty hunter are you?"

"I didn't think I was going to be uncuffing anyone."

"You never know when you'll come across someone," Vinnie said. "You should always have cuffs on you. This is why I'm losing money."

"You're on thin ice here," I said to Vinnie.

"I know," he said. "I'm sorry. It was nice of you to try to rescue me. You should get out before Snake comes back."

"Snake?"

"So sue me, that's his name. And he moves like a snake. He's creepy."

"I'm not leaving without you," I said. "Pull the chain tight."

I took my gun out, aimed it at the chain at short range, and pulled the trigger. The chain jumped and a link broke off. I rammed the gun back into my jeans, we ran to the other room, and just as we reached the door, Snake stepped over the threshold, gun drawn. His eyes flicked to Vinnie, and in that instant I whacked him in the head with the Maglite. He went to the floor on hands and knees, and I heard more men thundering up the stairs. I booted Snake out of the room, into the hall, slammed the door shut, and threw the bolt.

"Change in plans," I said to Vinnie. "Out the window."

Vinnie ran to the window, threw it open, and looked out. "Are you insane? We're four floors up."

"Fire escape," I said.

"It's rusted. It's junk!"

The door rattled, and a body slammed into it, but the bolt held.

"Go!" I said to Vinnie, shoving him out the window. "Go!"

The metal creaked under our weight, and chunks of metal flaked off when we ran down the stairs. No time to think about it.

"This is falling apart underneath me!" Vinnie yelled.

"Keep going!" I yelled back. "Don't stop."

We were on the third floor. I grabbed a railing for support, and the railing gave way. The fire escape groaned and separated from the building.

"Holy crap," Vinnie said. "Holy Mary, mother of God!"

The entire metal structure was disintegrating and collapsing into itself. We weren't exactly plummeting to the ground but rather sliding toward it. And then the

114

last bolt let go as we passed the second floor, and we were in a free fall. The framework crashed onto the black SUV, and Vinnie and I went flying off into space.

One of the men leaned out the fourth floor window and fired off a shot. Two more shots were fired from the alley not far from me. I was on my back, on the ground, all air knocked out of me. I was lifted to my feet and yanked toward the Jeep. It was Ranger. He had his hand clamped around my wrist, and he was running with me, half dragging me. We reached the Jeep, he hauled me up into the passenger seat, jumped in next to me, and spun the wheels taking off.

"Vinnie!" I said.

"Tank has him."

"I need to get Connie and Lula. They're on Stark Street."

Ranger turned the corner and cruised by the building. Connie and Lula were on the sidewalk looking like they were trying to stay calm, not having any luck at it. The door guard was gone. Probably on the fourth floor. Connie and Lula scrambled into the back of the Jeep, and Ranger moved off with a RangeMan SUV on his tail.

"So I guess that went well," Lula said.

Ranger slid a look at me. "Are you okay?"

I nodded. I was having a hard time finding words.

CHAPTER
TWELVE

Ranger took Connie and Lula to the office and waited while they got into their cars and drove away. The RangeMan SUV was still behind us, idling at the curb. Ranger called back and had Vinnie transferred up to the Jeep.

"Do I need to know why he's in his underwear?" Ranger asked me.

"That's how he was captured."

Vinnie climbed into the back, chain dangling from his handcuff, and Ranger took a universal handcuff key out of his pocket and handed it to Vinnie.

"I assume the first shot I heard was aimed at that chain," Ranger said to me.

"I didn't have a handcuff key."

"You're a bounty hunter," Ranger said. "You always carry handcuffs."

"I forgot, but I remembered my gun. And I whacked someone in the head with your Maglite."

Ranger smiled at me. "Babe."

"I guess I need to go home," Vinnie said.

"That's not a good idea," I told him. "Lucille isn't happy with you."

"She'll get over it," Vinnie said. "She always does."

Ranger was waiting for my instructions.

"Take him home," I said to Ranger.

Vinnie lived in a large yellow-and-white colonial in Pennington. It looked like a house a normal person would own, but it belonged to Vinnie. Go figure. Lucille made sure the lawn was mowed and the flowerbeds were mulched. White shears hung in the windows. It was close to eleven o'clock and lights were off in the house. The sky was overcast, and there was no moon. Some light filtered onto Lucille's lawn from a streetlight half a block away. It was enough light to see there was debris scattered across the yard.

Ranger pulled into the driveway, and Vinnie jumped out.

"What the heck?" Vinnie said, kicking through the debris. "This is my shirt. And socks." He walked to the door and rang the bell. He rang a second time. "Hey!" he yelled. "Hey, Lucille!"

A light flashed on in an upstairs window, the window opened, and Lucille stuck her head out. "Vinnie?"

"Yeah. I've been rescued. Let me in. I don't have my key."

"Your key won't do you any good, you jerk. I had the locks changed. Get your perverted butt off my lawn."

"This is my lawn, too," Vinnie said.

"The hell it is. My father bought this house for us, and it's in my name."

"It's common property, sweetie pie," Vinnie said. "And you'll have to kill me to get my half."

"No problem," Lucille said.

She disappeared from the window, and Vinnie started collecting his clothes. "I can't believe she did this," he said. "Look at this silk shirt laying here in the mulch. And my hand-painted tie."

Lucille reappeared in the window with a shotgun, and she blasted one off at Vinnie. "You're trespassing," she said.

"What are you gonna do, shoot me and call the police?" Vinnie yelled at her.

"No. I called my father. He's on his way over."

"Her father's dumped so many bodies in the landfill he has his own parking place," Ranger said.

Lucille squeezed off another shot, and Vinnie scrambled to the Jeep with his arms full of clothes.

Ranger put the Jeep in gear and backed out of the driveway. "Your call," he said to me.

"Take him to the office."

The black SUV was parked in front of the bonds office. There was a big gash in the hood and the roof was smashed in over the cargo area. A second car was parked behind it.

"Probably, we don't want to stop here," I said to Ranger.

"Give me a gun. I'll take care of those assholes," Vinnie said.

"You've caused enough trouble," I told him. "You're not getting a gun. And for crying out loud, put some clothes on. I'm going to have to disinfect the seat back there."

118

Ranger cut off Hamilton, into the Burg, and stopped at a cross street.

"I don't suppose you'd want to take him home with you," I said to Ranger.

Ranger glanced at Vinnie in the rearview mirror. "We could negotiate. The price would be high."

"Would I have to dress up like a geisha and rub your feet?"

Ranger cut his eyes to me. "It wasn't what I had in mind, but it would be a place to start."

"Cripes," Vinnie said. "You two want to get a room?"

"Tell me again why you rescued him," Ranger said.

I slid the Maglite back under the driver's seat. "Grandma Plum and Aunt Mim."

"Maybe he can stay with them," Ranger said.

"Unfortunately, that's not an option," I said. "He can stay with me tonight."

I gave Vinnie a quilt and a pillow. "You can spend one night here," I said. "One night. Tomorrow, you have to find a different place to live."

Vinnie dropped the quilt and pillow onto the couch. "I can't believe Lucille kicked me out."

"You were caught with a hooker!"

"I was doing Lucille a favor. She's a good woman, but she's picky about a lot of stuff. Don't do this, and don't do that. And what about me? I got needs. Okay, so I'm a pervert, but perverts got rights, too. There are places where I'd be considered normal. Borneo, maybe. Atlantic City."

Good grief. I was going to have to set off a roach bomb in my apartment after he left.

"Anyway, the big problem isn't Lucille," Vinnie said. "The big problem is Bobby Sunflower. You whacked one of his guys in the head, and you snatched me out from under him. He's not gonna like it."

"Would he have killed you if I hadn't gotten you out of there?"

"For sure. I was a dead man."

"All because you made some bad bets."

Vinnie remoted the television on, flipped through about twenty channels, and gave it up. "Sunflower's in trouble. He needs money, and he needs respect. He's in the middle of a war, and he can't show weakness."

"What war? Who's he fighting?"

"I don't know. Maybe I should go into therapy at one of those sex addiction places. Do you think that would get me off the hook?"

"Maybe with Lucille. I don't think Harry'll buy it."

My arm was scraped and the knee was torn out of my jeans from the fall. It would have been a lot worse if we hadn't crashed into the SUV. I limped out of the living room, closed the door on Vinnie, started to undress, and noticed I'd missed a call from Morelli on my cell phone.

"Hey," Morelli said when I called him back.

"Hey, yourself."

"Just checking to see if you're home. Shots were fired at Sunflower's apartment building tonight."

"Is that unusual?"

"Good point," Morelli said. "We also got a report of shots being fired from Vinnie's house. Lucille said she was shooting at a rat."

"That neighborhood's going to hell in a hand basket."

"Should I be worried?" Morelli asked me.

"Hard to say."

Morelli disconnected, and I limped into the bathroom, where I stood in the shower until all the rust was washed out of my hair. When I was done, I looked at the shampoo bottle. Empty. My refrigerator was also empty. I needed money. I needed to make another capture.

Vinnie was back to wearing only his underwear. He was in my kitchen, unshaven, his hair spiked up from sleep, his eyes half open.

"Where's the coffee?" he asked. "Where's the orange juice?"

"I don't have any," I told him. "I need to go shopping."

"I need coffee. Lucille always had my coffee ready."

"There's no Lucille," I told him. "Get used to it. And after today, there's no me. You can't stay here."

"Where will I go?"

"Stay with one of your friends."

"I don't have friends," Vinnie said. "I have hookers and bookies. And my bookie wants to shoot me."

"Do you have money?"

Vinnie flapped his arms. "Do I look like I have money? My wallet was left behind with my pants.

Maybe we should go back and check out the lawn in front of my house to see if Lucille tossed out cash and credit cards along with my clothes."

"What about the office? Don't you keep petty cash? Doesn't Connie have a corporate credit card?"

"We might have a small cash flow problem," Vinnie said.

"How small?"

"We might be a million in the red, give or take a couple bucks."

"What?"

"It's complicated," Vinnie said. "Book-keeping issues. We have too many outstanding skips."

"I have a stack of skips in my bag that I'm working on, but I don't think they add up to a million. And what about the bankers who underwrite you?"

"They aren't answering their phones."

Oh boy.

"You've got three minutes to get dressed," I said to Vinnie. "I'm taking you to my parents' house. When they get fed up with you, I'll think of something else. At least you can get coffee there before my mother kicks you out."

I debated calling ahead but decided against it. If I dumped him on my mother's doorstep and drove away real fast, she'd have to take him in, at least for a while. If I called, she could say no.

Twenty minutes later, I idled in front of my parents' house while Vinnie walked to the front door. On the rare possibility that no one was home, I didn't want to just drive off. He didn't have a cell phone to call me to come back. I saw the front door open and I laid rubber.

I drove by the office twice before I parked. I didn't see the bashed-in SUV, and I didn't see any angry-looking guys hanging out with guns drawn, so I figured things were quiet this morning. Connie was at her desk. Lula hadn't arrived.

"You didn't bring Vinnie with you, did you?" Connie asked. "I already had a visit from Bobby Sunflower this morning."

I poured myself a cup of coffee. "He gets up early."

"I guess he was motivated. He wants his money or he wants Vinnie. He said if he didn't get either of those things by Friday he was going to eliminate the office."

"Eliminate it?"

"Like from the face of the earth."

"Could be worse," I said. "According to Vinnie, this office is about a million in the red."

Connie froze for a beat. "Vinnie said that?"

"Yeah. Didn't you know?"

"I don't do the books. Vinnie has an accountant for that."

"Maybe we should talk to the accountant."

"The accountant's dead. He got run over by a truck last week. Twice."

"That's not good."

"No," Connie said. "It's really not good."

"Does Sunflower know we were the ones to spring Vinnie?"

"Yeah, but I think it's too embarrassing to let go public. And I think he'd rather have the money than to see us shot full of holes."

I drank some coffee and took a doughnut from the box on Connie's desk. "So we need to raise money."

"It's up to a million two."

"Chopper is a pretty high-bond. The toilet paper guy isn't worth much, but he might be easy to capture."

"Butch Goodey is worth something," Connie said.

"I thought he skipped to Mexico."

"I heard he got back last week, and he's working at the meat-packing plant."

Butch Goodey is 6'6" tall and weighs about three hundred pounds. He's wanted for exposing himself to thirteen women over a period of two days. He said they were lucky to get to see Mr Magic, and he blamed it on a sex-enhancement drug that gave him a thirty-two-hour erection. The judge who set Goodey's bond asked for the name of the drug, wrote it on a piece of paper, and slipped the paper into his pocket.

"I'll put Goodey at the head of the list," I said.

Lula swung into the office. "At the head of what list?"

"The catch 'em list," I told her. "We need to make money today."

"So we're going after Butch Goodey? I thought he was in Mexico."

"He's back. He's working at the meat-packing plant."

"I hate that place," Lula said. "It gives me the creeps. You drive by with your windows open, and you can hear cows mooing. You're only supposed to hear stuff like that on a farm. I mean, what the heck's the world coming to when you can hear cows mooing in Trenton? And who the heck would work at a meat-packing plant anyway?"

"Butch Goodey," I said.

The meat-packing plant was down by the river, south of town, on the edge of a residential area that was blue-collar or no-collar. It took up half a block, with some of that space devoted to holding pens, where the cattle went in, and some to loading docks, where the hamburger meat came out.

At nine-thirty in the morning, the plant was in full swing.

It was going to be a glorious, sunny, warm day and the area around the plant smelled faintly of cow.

"You know what this makes me think about?" Lula said, jumping down from the Jeep, standing in the parking lot. "It makes me think I could use a new leather handbag. If we get done early today, we should go to the mall."

I didn't think we were going to get done early. I expected this was going to be a very long day. It was Thursday, and there was no way we could get all of the money by bringing in a few skips. If we didn't come up with over a million dollars by tomorrow, Grandma Plum and Aunt Mim were going to be wearing black.

CHAPTER
THIRTEEN

Lula and I entered a small reception area and approached the woman at the front desk. I gave her my business card and told her I wanted to speak to Butch Goodey. The woman ran her finger down a roster of names attached to a clipboard and located Goodey.

"He's helping unload cattle right now," she said. "The easiest way to find him would be to go around the building from the outside. Just go out the door, turn left, and keep walking. You'll see an area around the corner where trucks are off-loading, and Butch should be there."

"I'm glad we didn't have to go through the building," Lula said, "because I don't want to see them chopping up cows. I like thinking meat grows in the supermarket."

We turned the corner and came to an area where cattle were milling around in a pen.

"What kind of cows do you suppose these are?" Lula asked. "Are these hamburger cows or steak cows?"

"I don't know," I said. "All cows pretty much look the same to me."

"Yeah, but some are bigger than others and some got horns. These cows are hefty black cows. I guess they're my kind of cow," Lula said.

I had a photo of Butch. I'd tried to find him before he skipped to Mexico, so I had some idea of what I was looking for, and at 6'6" and three hundred pounds, he shouldn't be that hard to spot. I scanned the holding area and picked him out, standing a foot taller than everyone else. He was watching over a gate that fed the cattle from a pen to a ramp that led into the building.

I had cuffs tucked into the back of my jeans, but I wasn't sure they were big enough to fit around Butch's wrists. I had FlexiCuffs hooked onto a belt loop, but it was hard to be sneaky with FlexiCuffs. My hope was that I could talk him into going downtown with me to re-up for his court hearing.

"Stay here by the cattle truck," I said to Lula. "I don't want to spook Butch by having both of us come at him. I'm going to circle around and try to talk to him."

"Sure," Lula said. "What do you want me to do if he bolts and runs?"

"Tackle him and cuff him," I said.

"Okey-dokey."

Butch was feeding the cattle one by one onto the ramp, concentrating on his job. I skirted the holding pen, moving behind an empty cattle truck, and I came up behind him. I had my cuff in my hand, taking measure of his gargantuan wrist, when he turned and saw me.

"You!" he said. "I know you. You're the bounty hunter."

"Yes, but . . ."

"I'm not going to jail. You can't make me. It wasn't my fault."

Butch jumped into the pen with the stupefied cows and ran for the gate by the truck. Lula saw him coming at her, opened the gate to tackle him, and the rest was the stuff nightmares are made of. When the gate creaked open, every cow picked its head up and sniffed freedom. Butch went through the gate first, knocking Lula on her ass against the fence. Butch was followed by a cow stampede. The cows galloped out of the pen, into the parking lot, and scattered. In a matter of seconds, not a single cow could be seen.

Truck drivers and cow wranglers stood open-mouthed, frozen in place for a full minute.

"What the bejeezus was that?" someone finally said.

Lula hauled herself to her feet and adjusted her purse on her shoulder. "I'm gonna sue someone," she said. "I could have been killed. I'm lucky I wasn't stampeded on. This cow plant is negligent. I'm calling my lawyer."

"You were the one who opened the gate," I told her.

"Yeah, but they should have had a lock on it so I couldn't do that. And what are we doing with cows in Trenton anyway? How many times do I have to ask that question?"

Someone screamed half a block away, and I heard the sound of cow feet clomping down a street somewhere. Men were pouring out of the plant, organizing search teams. A big black cow trotted into the lot, three men took off after it, and the cow ran away, headed for the 7-Eleven on Broad.

"Well, I guess our business is done here," Lula said. "Now what?"

"Now we ride around and try to spot Butch."

And we get out of the parking lot before someone remembers Lula was the one who opened the gate.

"I kind of worked up an appetite being around all those cows," Lula said, climbing into the Jeep. "I wouldn't mind getting a burger."

I plugged the key into the ignition. "After we find Butch."

"What are we gonna do if we find him?" Lula wanted to know. "Are you gonna run him over with the Jeep? Looks to me like that's the only way you'll catch him. He's as big as one of those cows."

I drove out of the lot, turned at the corner, and stopped to let a cow cross the street in front of me.

"I bet this happens all the time," Lula said. "These people are probably used to having cows in their yards. It's probably like living next to the jail. I bet there's people escaping from the jail all the time, too."

Anything was possible, but for all the time I've lived in Trenton, which was all my life, I've never heard of cows making a run for it out of the packing plant.

Two cop cars raced through an intersection one street over. I could hear men shouting to one another, and I heard a cow bellow not far off. A man bolted from between two houses with a cow hot on his heels. The guy scrambled on top of a car, and the cow ran off in another direction.

I doubled back to the plant and spotted Butch getting into his car. The lot was filled with crazed cows and crazed cow catchers, so I decided to follow Butch and attempt a capture somewhere else.

Butch took Broad to Hamilton, found his way to Cluck-in-a-Bucket, and went straight to the drive-thru window. He was driving a white Taurus that was a bunch of years old. Easy to follow.

"This is enough to give me religion," Lula said. "How good is this? We follow some idiot to Cluck-in-a-Bucket. Just when I'm hungry, too. I bet it's the bottle. You got your bottle, right?"

"Yeah."

"I knew it," Lula said. "The bottle's working for us."

Butch put his order in, pulled up to the next window, and I hung back.

"I got a order," Lula said to me. "Pull up to the window."

"I'm not getting stuck in the drive-thru. If he parks, you can go inside and get your order while I make the capture. If he leaves with his food, you'll have to wait."

"Okay, I could do that," Lula said. "That sounds like a plan."

Butch got his food and parked nose-in, facing the side of the building. Lula jumped out of the Jeep and hustled inside, and I parked directly behind Butch, blocking his exit. My first choice was to talk to him and convince him to come downtown with me. My second choice was to give him a shot with my stun gun and handcuff him to his car. Then I'd pay a tow truck to drag him to the police station. I'd still be way ahead. Ordinarily, I'd stun a guy and Lula and I would wrestle him into my back seat. Since Butch was three hundred pounds soaking wet, wrestling wasn't practical.

I trotted up to the Taurus and bent to talk to Butch. He jumped at my voice, a piece of burger fell out of his mouth, and he shrieked like a girl.

"I just want to talk to you," I said.

"I'm not going to jail!" he yelled at me.

He threw the Taurus into reverse, I hit him once with the stun gun, and he twitched and squeaked, but that was it. The Taurus plowed into Ranger's Jeep and knocked it back about ten feet, totally bashing in the entire left side. Butch slammed the Taurus into drive, jumped the sidewalk, made a sharp turn, and took off out of the lot.

Lula sashayed out with two bags of food and stood looking at the Jeep. "You're in trouble," she said. "You wrecked Ranger's Jeep." She looked around. "Where's Butch?"

"Gone."

"He must be a real fast eater."

"I walked up to his car, and he panicked. I hit him with the stun gun, and it had no effect."

"No shit," Lula said. "You need a cattle prod for him."

I hauled my cell phone out and dialed Ranger.

"Babe," he said.

"Bad news," I told him. "I sort of wrecked your Jeep."

"It was only a matter of time," he said. And he disconnected.

Five minutes later, a RangeMan SUV drove into the parking lot. Hal and another guy got out, looked at the Jeep, and smiled.

"No disrespect," Hal said to me, "but you've done better."

This was true. I was driving Ranger's Porsche one time, and it got smashed flat as a pancake by a garbage truck. Hard to top that.

"Raphael will take care of the Jeep," Hal said. "And I'm at your disposal. Where would you ladies like to go?"

"The bonds office," I told him. "We need to regroup."

"How'd it go?" Connie asked. "Did you catch anyone?"

"Nope," Lula said. "But we trashed Ranger's Jeep. And we did some other stuff, but I might not want to talk about it."

Connie gave me raised eyebrows.

"Lula opened a gate at the packing plant and set a whole bunch of cows loose," I said. "They're probably in Bordentown by now."

"They were like *Born Free* cows," Lula said.

"We aren't doing so good in the money-raising department," Connie said.

I slouched in the orange chair in front of her desk. "Maybe we should call the police."

"Or we could ship Vinnie off to Brazil," Lula said. "We could put him in nitwit protection."

My phone rang, and I groaned when I saw the number. It was my mother.

"When are you picking him up?" my mother wanted to know.

"Who?"

"You know who! He's in your father's chair, watching television, drinking coffee."

"Lucille kicked him out."

"Good for her," my mother said. "I'd kick him out, too, but I can't get him out of the chair. When are you coming to get him?"

"Here's the thing," I said to my mother. "He doesn't have anyplace to stay."

"He can't stay here. And I swear I'll never make you another pineapple upside-down cake if you don't get him out of here."

"I'll be right there." I grabbed my tote bag and stood. "We have to get Vinnie," I said to Lula. "My mother's done with him."

"You can't bring him back here," Connie said.

"Can I put him in your house?"

"Not even for a moment."

I looked at Lula.

"Nuh-uh," Lula said. "I don't even like him. And soon as he's left alone, he'll be tryin' all my special dresses on." Lula's attention moved to the plateglass window in the front of the office. "It's the Moon Man," she said.

Mooner pushed the door open and gave us the peace sign. "Ladies," he said. "How goes it?"

"It goes okay," I said. "How goes it with you?"

"I don't know. I think they might have put some wacky mushrooms on my pizza last night. I was driving down Broad Street just now, and I swear I thought a cow was walking down the street."

"Hunh," Lula said. "That's crazy, all right."

"Some cows got loose at the packing plant this morning," I told Mooner.

Mooner clapped a hand to his heart. "That's a mega relief. Last time I saw cows walking down the street, I had to go into rehab."

"What were you doing on Broad?" I asked him.

"I was handing out fliers. I got some for you, too." Mooner put a stack of papers on Connie's desk. "The Alliance is having its annual Hobbit Con, and I'm in charge this year. It's an awesome honor."

"I've never been to a Hobbit Con," Lula said. "What do you do there?"

"You dress up like a Hobbit," Mooner said. "And you get a Hobbit name. And there's all kinds of Hobbit food. And there are Hobbit games. And Hobbit music."

"I might like that," Lula said, taking a flier off Connie's desk and reading it. "I'm always open to new experiences. Do you got a Hobbit name?" Lula asked him.

"Bungo Goodchild," Mooner said.

"I could see that," Lula said. "What would my name be?"

"You could be Alvyan Jumpswell of Fair Downs," Mooner said. "And Connie could be Primula Boffin."

"What if I don't want to be Primula Boffin?" Connie said.

"What about Stephanie?" Lula wanted to know. "What's her Hobbit name?"

"Ysellyra Thorney."

"Yeah, she looks like a Ysellyra Thorney," Lula said.

"I have a problem," I said to Mooner. "Vinnie's wife kicked him out of the house, and he hasn't got any place to stay. Do you suppose you could babysit him for me this afternoon and maybe tonight?"

"Whoa, I'd be honored," Mooner said. "Vinnie's the dude. He's like famous. He runs ASC."

"What's ASC?" I asked Mooner.

"Alternative Sex Convention. It's like cutting-edge."

"That's a shocker," Connie said.

"Yeah," Mooner said. "ASC is huge. Maybe Vinnie can give me some pointers."

"Unless you got Hobbits that wear chaps and nothin' else, you probably don't want any of Vinnie's pointers," Lula said.

"Do you remember where my parents live?" I asked Mooner.

"Yep. I could find it with my eyes closed."

I wrote the address on the back of my card and gave it to Mooner. "Just in case," I said. "Call me if there are problems. Don't let Vinnie out of your sight, and stay away from Stark Street."

Mooner ambled out of the office, and moments later, we heard a backfire and the Moon Bus chugged down the street.

"Do you think you can trust him to keep Vinnie under wraps?" Lula asked me.

"If Vinnie wants to stay alive, he'll make sure he stays hidden."

I called my parents' house and asked for Vinnie.

135

"Mooner is coming to get you," I told Vinnie. "He's going to let you stay in his RV. Do not leave the RV!"

I glanced at my watch. "It's coming up to lunchtime," I said to Lula. "Let's look for Chopper."

"What about Butch?" Connie wanted to know.

"I need an address. I doubt he'll go back to work. And if I'm going to get him, I need to do it fast. He doesn't want to go to jail. He's going to run again."

CHAPTER
FOURTEEN

Lula and I left the bonds office, and Lula looked up
and down the street. "I thought for sure there'd be a
new black car delivered by now," Lula said. "You don't
suppose Ranger ran out of cars, do you?"

"Maybe I've reached my monthly quota."

A green SUV pulled in behind Lula's Firebird, and
Morelli got out.

"I'll be with you in a minute," I told Lula, and I went
to meet Morelli.

Morelli stepped close to me, hands at my waist, and
he nuzzled my neck.

"Is this a social visit?" I asked him.

"Not entirely. I wanted to see if you smelled like
cow."

I stepped away and looked at him. "Well?"

"Nope."

"Is it against the law to smell like cow?"

"It is if you let a herd of them loose in the city."

"How did you know?"

"Several of the workers who were interviewed
remembered seeing a black woman with red hair and
big boobs and a pretty girl with a brown ponytail."

"They thought I was pretty?"

"Everyone thinks you're pretty," Morelli said.

"How about you?"

"Especially me," he said. "What the hell were you doing at the packing plant?"

"I was after Butch Goodey. And it was all an accident."

"You accidentally started a stampede?"

"Not me, exactly. Butch was working the holding pen, and he panicked when he saw me. And he bolted. And the cows bolted with him."

Morelli put his hand to his chest. "Heartburn," he said. "You have any Rolaids?"

"Too much stress," I said. "It's your job."

"It's not my job. It's you. You're a magnet for disaster."

"So find a new girlfriend. Some nice, boring woman who remembers to buy bread."

"Maybe I will," Morelli said.

"Fine!"

"Fine, yourself."

"Hmmph," I said, and I turned on my heel, marched back to Lula's Firebird, and got in.

"That looked like it went well," Lula said.

"Just drive."

"Don't be Miss Crankypants with me just because you aren't gettin' any."

"I could get plenty if I wanted."

"You know what your problem is? You got too many scruples. One or two scruples is okay, but you get too many of them, and it clogs everything up."

What she said made no sense at all, but was probably right.

"I got some scruples," Lula said, "but I know when to stop. There's a point where you have to say enough is enough and screw scruples."

"Is this conversation going somewhere?"

"If it was me, I'd sleep with both of them, and when they found out, I'd move on. Sayonara, sweetie."

"Jeez."

Lula looked over at me. "Maybe that don't work for you."

I sprang forward in my seat. "It's him! Chopper just drove past us. Black Lexus, tinted windows, fancy wheels, and his plate starts with CH."

"I'm on it," Lula said. "Keep your eye on him."

There were three cars between us. Traffic was moderate on Hamilton at this time of the day.

"He turned right on Chambers," I said to Lula.

"He's going for one of his burger places," Lula said. "I bet he's heading for Meat & Go. It's just ahead."

We lost sight of the Lexus on Chambers, but spotted it parked at Meat & Go. Chopper was a big-ticket bond, and I was tired of getting skunked. No way was this one getting away.

"Park behind him so he's blocked," I said to Lula.

"What are you, nuts? This is my baby. I'm not getting my baby rammed. We saw what happened with Ranger's Jeep. I'm parking far away, where no one's gonna park next to me and ding my door."

"Okay, fine," I said. "Just park."

We got out of the Firebird and took inventory. Lula had cuffs, pepper spray, stun gun, Glock, pearl-handled Derringer, switchblade knife, and brass knuckles. I had my .45, cuffs, pepper spray, and stun gun. Lula wanted to use everything in her arsenal. I wanted to use nothing.

"No excessive force," I said to her.

"Sure, I know that," Lula said. "Just get outta my way. I'm gonna bag this idiot."

"No! Let me talk to him. He's a professional. He'll cooperate."

"You always say that, and then they run over your toes."

I put my hand to my chest and grunted.

"Something wrong?" Lula wanted to know.

"I think I have heartburn. What does heartburn feel like?"

"Pain."

"I've got it. Do you have Rolaids?"

"No. I never have trouble with heartburn on account of I keep a positive attitude. And I got good digestion from eating right."

"You eat everything."

"Exactly. I get variety in my diet. Even when I was on that one diet, which I'm not anymore, I made the most of it."

This was true.

"Stay behind me," I said to Lula. "I'm going in."

I had the cuffs at easy access, and I had the stun gun in hand. True, it didn't work on Butch, but that was a fluke. I crossed the lot and rapped on the tinted driver's side window. The window rolled down, and Chopper looked out at me. I knew Chopper by sight. He looked like Joe Pesci, if Joe Pesci was Cuban.

"Mortimer Gonzolez?" I asked.

"Yeah. What about it?"

"Bond enforcement," I said. "You need to come with me to set a new court date."

Technically, this was correct, but mostly it was baloney. He needed to come with me so he could get locked up until someone came to bond him out again. And bonding him out would cost him more money.

"Bite me," Chopper said. And he powered his window up.

"That went well," Lula said.

"If you say that one more time, I'm going to hit you with the stun gun and spray you full of pepper spray," I said to her.

Lula pointed her Glock at Chopper's front tire and fired off four rounds. The driver's side door flew open and Chopper lunged out and looked at his tire and looked at Lula.

"Are you fuckin' nuts?" Chopper yelled. "Do you know what one of them tires costs? It's not no ordinary fuckin' tire. It's a run-flat."

I clapped a bracelet onto his wrist, and he took a swing at me. I ducked and zapped him with the stun gun. Chopper's eyes went blank, and he dropped to the pavement.

"I think we finally got one," Lula said.

I snapped the second bracelet onto Chopper, and Lula and I dragged him to the Firebird.

"Watch that you don't get his shoes onto my leather upholstery," Lula said. "I just had it detailed."

We hefted Chopper onto the back seat and did a high five.

"This is what I'm talking about," Lula said, getting into the Firebird. "We're on a roll now. It's the bottle. You got it, right?"

I slid onto the passenger seat and clicked my seat belt in place. "It's in my shoulder bag."

Lula drove two blocks and pulled into a convenience store lot. "I got a idea. The bottle's working for us, right?"

"I guess."

"Here's what we're gonna do. We're gonna go get a lottery ticket while we're hot. I bet you anything we win a ton of money."

"Who's paying for the ticket?"

"You," Lula said.

"I don't think so."

"I spent my last twenty on burgers." Lula looked in the rearview mirror. "I bet Chopper got money."

"Don't even think about it."

Lula unsnapped her seat belt and lurched out of the car. "It's just borrowing. I'll pay him back right away with our winnings."

"What if we don't win?"

"Of course we'll win. You got the bottle." Lula leaned over Chopper and came out with his wallet. She took a twenty and stuffed the wallet back into Chopper's jacket pocket. "We're just borrowing," she told Chopper. "We'll be right back."

142

"There's no we," I said. "I want no part of this."

"There you go with the scruples again. You gotta learn a real scruple from a worthless scruple."

"We don't steal from people we capture."

"Borrow," Lula said. "We're borrowing. And it's for a good cause. That always makes a difference."

I had my arms crossed over my chest, holding firm.

"You're gonna have to get out of the car and come with me," Lula said. "You're the one with the lucky bottle. And besides, I'm not getting back behind the wheel until we do this. And I'm gonna hold my breath, too."

"Oh, for Pete's sake!" I said, unsnapping my seat belt. I got out of the car, slammed the door, and stomped into the store.

"We want lottery tickets," Lula said to the clerk. "Here's our borrowed twenty, which is okay because we got a lucky bottle. And we haven't got time for the Powerball. We're gonna take those five-dollar scratch things."

Lula took her tickets and stepped back and started scratching. Nothing on the first ticket. Nothing on the second ticket. Nothing on the third ticket.

"This is it," Lula said. "I can feel it. This here's the lucky ticket." She scratched the ticket and shrieked. "I won! I won! I knew I'd win. What did I tell you?"

I looked over her shoulder. "How much did you win?"

"Ten dollars."

"I don't want to rain on your parade, but you spent twenty to win ten."

"Yeah, but I won. We need more money, now that we're on a roll. This is just the beginning."

"We haven't got more money."

"Chopper has money. His wallet was full of money. We just need to borrow more."

"No!"

"Yeah, but how are we going to pay him back if we don't borrow more?"

"I'll mail it to him," I said.

Lula handed her lottery ticket in and got her ten dollars.

"Hold on," Lula said. "I need a cookie. I got a cookie craving." Lula went to the cookie aisle and came back with a bunch of bags and boxes.

"That's twelve-fifty," the clerk said.

Lula looked at me.

I blew out a sigh, dug into my purse, and came up with two dollars and change.

"Now we can celebrate our winnings," Lula said.

We took our cookies and went back to the Firebird.

"What the heck?" Lula said.

No Chopper.

"Did we put him in the trunk and I forgot?" Lula asked.

"He's on foot, probably trying to get back to his car. Maybe we can catch him."

Lula peeled out of the lot and drove the two blocks to Meat & Go. The black Lexus SUV was gone.

"Yeah, but you gotta look on the bright side," Lula said. "We won the lottery."

I took a package of Hostess Snowballs out of the plastic bag and stuffed one into my mouth.

"See if you can find him," I said to Lula.

We cruised the other lunch locations, and Lula did a loop past Chopper's apartment. No Lexus SUV parked there, either. He was most likely somewhere getting my cuffs removed.

"No disrespect intended. And I don't mean to blaspheme your bottle. But I'm starting to think it sucks as a lucky bottle," Lula said.

I was glad she felt that way, because between the bottle and my Smith & Wesson, my shoulder bag was giving me a neck cramp. I'd be more than happy to leave them home tomorrow.

Connie called on my cell phone. "I have some information on Butch Goodey," she said.

I hoped the information was that he was seen boarding a plane for Antarctica. It wouldn't bother me if I never saw Butch Goodey ever again. It was like trying to capture King Kong.

"I have a current address off his employment record, and I have siblings. You should have the siblings on his original bond document," Connie said.

A current address. Crap. I hung up and slumped in my seat.

"What?" Lula wanted to know.

"Connie has a current address for Butch."

"Crap," Lula said. "I'm not liking any of these people we gotta catch. They're too big and sneaky. And no one wants to get caught. On the other hand, the big dummy knocked me over, and I got a smudge on my skirt. I'm gonna have to take it to the cleaners. He should pay for that."

"He lives on Keene Street, in one of those little row houses."

"I'm on it," Lula said.

CHAPTER
FIFTEEN

The white Taurus was parked at the curb in front of
Butch's row house. Originally, these were company
houses for a company that made porcelain pipe. They
were single-story, twelve units hooked together, maroon
asbestos shingle roof and siding. No yard. No porch,
front or back. Street parking. A little bleak, but the
plumbing worked in almost all of them.

"We need a plan," Lula said. "I don't want to get
knocked on my ass again."

"The stun gun doesn't work on him, so I'll ring the
bell, and when he answers, I'll give him a blast with
pepper spray. We'll both step back to let the spray settle,
and then we'll wrap the FlexiCuffs on him."

"If I have to shoot him, I'll shoot him in the foot,"
Lula said.

"No shooting!"

"You always say that."

"Shooting isn't good. It hurts people. It could get
you in jail."

Lula had her lower lip stuck out. Eyes narrowed. "He
made me smudge my skirt."

"You don't shoot someone over a smudged skirt."

"I was only gonna shoot him in the foot."

The pain was back in my chest. I burped and it went away.

"You got a digestive issue," Lula said.

"I never had this problem before."

"It's probably that you're gettin' old," Lula said. "Things like that happen to you when you get old. Or maybe you're pregnant. Oops, hold on, you're not pregnant, on account of you're not gettin' any."

"Could we please concentrate on the problem at hand, which is capturing Sasquatch?"

"Sure," Lula said. "I could do that."

We walked to the door, and I rang the bell. I had pepper spray in hand, ready to use. Lula was positioned behind me. After a moment, the door opened and Butch stared out at us, looking like a giant in his tiny house.

"Shit!" he said.

I gave him a face full of spray and jumped back. He bellowed and thrashed around, flailing his arms, his eyes squinched shut. "Ow!" he yelled. "Owwwww!"

I was jumping around, trying to grab a wrist. "Get hold of him," I said to Lula. "Get an arm."

"I can't fuckin' get an arm," Lula said. "He won't stand still."

Butch lashed out, his eyes still closed, knocked Lula back about ten feet, and charged past me like a raging bull.

"Arrrrrgh!" he screamed. "Gaaaaah!"

His nose was running and his eyes were streaming tears, but nothing was stopping him. He ran out the door, down the sidewalk, and took off. I ran flat out after him, yelling for Lula to help. I chased him half a block, and he turned the corner, crossed the street, and cut through a backyard. I could hear Lula pounding behind me, breathing hard. I wasn't exactly breathing easy, either, and I was thinking it might have been better to let Lula shoot him in the foot, because I had no idea what I was going to do if I caught him.

He came to a privacy fence, stopped dead in his tracks, and I slammed into him and held fast. Lula came up behind me and grabbed him, and we all toppled over and went to the ground. My fear now was that Butch and Lula would roll on top of me and I'd be crushed flat as a pancake. We scrabbled around, with Butch struggling to get to his feet and Lula and me hanging on for dear life.

"Cuff 'im!" Lula was yelling. "Kick 'im in the nuts. Poke out his eyeball."

I was trying, but I wasn't having a lot of luck. He was too big, too heavy, too strong, too freaked out over jail. I made an attempt to slip the plastic FlexiCuffs on him, and he flicked me away like I was a bug. I was thrown a couple feet and landed on black court shoes attached to long legs clad in black cargo pants. Ranger. He gave me a hand and pulled me up. "We need to talk," he said.

"Help," Lula said. "Get this clown off me. I can't breathe."

"Let go," Butch said to Lula. "Let go of me."

Ranger waded in and separated them. Butch scrambled to his feet and was ready to run.

"Stay," Ranger said to him.

Butch immediately went still. Ranger took the cuffs from me and secured Butch.

"How do you do that?" I asked Ranger.

"I speak with authority."

"Can you teach me to do that?"

"No," Ranger said.

He called for backup on his cell phone, took Butch by the arm, and walked him to the street. Ranger's Porsche Turbo was parked at the curb.

"How did you find me?" I asked him.

"I called Connie, and she gave me Goodey's address. I was on the street, and you ran past me."

"I didn't see you."

"You had your eye on the prize."

Lula was following behind us, adjusting her skirt and rearranging her boobs. "This must be Knock Lula On Her Ass Day," she said. "I don't know why I try to look professional. I'm either fallin' down stairs, or rollin' around with cows, or wrestlin' with idiots, getting my nice clothes all wrecked. I might just as well come to work wearin' a garbage bag."

Ranger smiled but didn't say anything.

"And I saw that smile," Lula said to Ranger. "You better not be laughin' at me."

"It would be a crime against humanity to see you dressed in a garbage bag," Ranger said.

"Hunh," Lula said. "Are you tryin' to sweet talk me?"

"Yes," Ranger said.

"I guess it's working," Lula told him.

150

"I assume you need a car," Ranger said to me. "I can have one of my men bring Goodey downtown for you, and you can come back to RangeMan and pick something out . . . again."

"I'm happy to hear that," Lula said. "Because I need to go home and make a wardrobe adjustment."

Five minutes later, the RangeMan SUV pulled to the curb and collected Goodey. I got into the Turbo next to Ranger and relaxed back in the seat.

"Word on the street is that Bobby Sunflower scammed money from the wrong man," Ranger said.

"Some other bad guy?"

"That's the vibe I'm getting. Sunflower makes a lot of his money by blackmailing and extorting honest businessmen into stealing from their clients. The owners get involved with him and are forced to cook their books. When the business finally collapses and their creditors and clients come looking, Bobby's evaporated. It's standard Mob procedure. All money is drained from the legitimate business, and the original owners are left holding the bag. They're the guys who go to jail, jump off bridges, or blow their brains out. It sounds like this time Sunflower bulldozed the wrong company and stepped on some powerful toes."

"Does this connect to me?"

Ranger crossed Hamilton and rolled into the center of the city. "It might. If Sunflower had a grip on Vinnie's business to the extent that there's nothing left but bleached bones, someone could end up going to jail, and it wouldn't be Sunflower."

"Is there a way out for Vinnie?"

"I don't know. I don't know how involved he is with the bad guys. I think he was snatched because Sunflower is desperate for money, and he thought Vinnie was a golden goose. He was counting on Harry to pony up."

"But Harry wouldn't do it."

"No. Now Sunflower's stuck in a bad spot. If he doesn't get the money, not only does he lose respect, but he probably dies."

Ranger turned a corner, drove half a block, pulled into RangeMan's underground garage, and he parked in his reserved spot in front of the elevator. Ranger had four spots for his personal vehicles. He currently had the Porsche Turbo, a Porsche Cayenne, and a customized F150 truck. A shiny black Mercedes SUV with fancy wheels was in the fourth space. I was hoping it was mine.

Ranger shut the Porsche down. "If you looked at me with half as much longing as you're looking at that Mercedes, I'd take you upstairs and make you wish you never had to leave my bed."

"Is the Mercedes for me?" I asked.

"Yes."

"And the bed . . . I'd have to leave eventually, wouldn't I?"

"Yes," Ranger said.

"Why do you give me cars?"

"It's fun," Ranger said. "And it keeps you safe. Do you want to know why keeping you safe is important to me?"

"You love me?"

"Yes."

A sigh inadvertently escaped. "We're really screwed up, aren't we?"

"In a very large way," Ranger said.

He slid his arm across my seat back, leaned forward, and kissed me. He ended the kiss, and our eyes held. And I was pretty sure he knew he'd smoked the Mercedes he'd given me.

I parked my new car in front of the bonds office and went inside.

"Where's Lula?" Connie asked.

"She went home to change. The little skirt wasn't working."

"Looks like you got a new car."

"It's a loaner from Ranger."

"I hope you thanked him."

"I'm running a tab," I told her.

My cell phone rang, and I picked it up to Ranger.

"Bad news," Ranger said. "Goodey didn't make it to the station. He got carsick on the way, and when the guys stopped to help him, he managed to get loose from the FlexiCuffs, hijack the SUV, and take off."

"You're kidding."

"I wish," Ranger said. "We got the SUV back, but no Goodey." And he disconnected.

A shadow slid over the office when the afternoon sun was blotted out by the hulking carcass of Mooner's RV parking behind my Mercedes.

"Greetings, Hobbits Primula Boffin and Ysellyra Thorney," Mooner said, ambling in. "How fare thee?"

153

Mooner was dressed in a T-shirt advertising beer, red capri pants, flip-flops, and a brown cape. Looked to me like a cross between a stoner and a Hobbit.

"It fares good," I said. "How fares it with you?"

"It's faring excellent. Doderick Bracegirdle was, like, mucho helpful with Hobbit Con."

"Doderick Bracegirdle?"

"Formerly known as Vinnie," Mooner said. "The dude is genius. He, like, came up with this awesome game. Toss the Cockring over the Dildo. It'll be a wowser with all the Hobbit lovers. The problem is maintaining an authenticity level. Being that Hobbits are, like . . . little, the dildo would have to be size appropriate."

Lula pushed the front door open. "What about a dildo?"

"Mooner wants to have a cockring toss at Hobbit Con, and he's thinking the dildo would have to be Hobbit-size."

"Yeah, that makes sense," Lula said. "You need a Hobbit dildo store."

"I looked in the Yellow Pages," Mooner said. "Nada."

"I imagine it's a specialty item," Lula said. "You probably have to Google it. Or maybe you could look on eBay."

"Whoa," Mooner said. "Brilliant."

"Probably, you don't want to leave the RV in front of the office for too long with Vinnie in it," Connie said to Mooner.

"No problemo," Mooner said. "Vinnie isn't in it."

My breath caught in my chest. "Where is he?"

154

"I don't know," Mooner said. "My man took off. I thought we were groovin', you know? And then next thing, I turn around and no Doderick. Heck, I guess that's genius for you, right? In the wind, man."

"Back up. Where were you when he disappeared?"

"I was at the bakery on Nottingway. I was leaving fliers for Hobbit Con, and I got to talking with the pastry lady. They've got, like, some serious treats in there. Anyway, when I came out of the bakery, the mobile mansion was without the duder."

"Did he leave a note? Was anything out of place? Was there blood?"

"Negative, negative, negative."

"Did you see anyone in the parking lot? Any cars?"

"I think there was an SUV and a really cool sports car."

"A Ferrari?"

"Yeah, or it might have been a Corvette."

"Which?"

"I had a lot on my mind. I was thinking about the ring toss, and I was entering the sugar zone. I'm not sure about the car. I mean, all that frosting . . ."

I felt sick inside. I was trying to help Vinnie, and I was completely inept. I should have insisted we go to the police. I should have told Morelli. I should have asked Ranger for help. I should have shipped Vinnie off to Miami.

"This don't sound good," Lula said. "Sunflower drives a Ferrari." She looked at Mooner. "Did the SUV have a bashed-in roof?"

"I don't think so."

"Let's not panic," Connie said. "Lots of people drive an SUV."

"Yeah," Lula said. "And lots of people drive fancy sports cars that might look like a Ferrari."

"Are you sure he's not in the RV?" I asked Mooner. "Maybe he decided to take a nap in a closet or something."

"I thought of that," Mooner said, "but I couldn't find him."

CHAPTER
SIXTEEN

"Do you have a phone number for Mickey Gritch?"
I asked Connie.

Connie dialed Mickey and gave me her headset.

"Yeah?" Mickey said.

"It's Stephanie Plum," I told him. "I was wondering if there were any new developments."

"You gotta give me more than that," he said. "Do you want to bet on a horse? Do you want to know if Sunflower collected insurance on his bashed-in SUV? Do you need a hooker?"

"Actually, I was wondering if you heard anything about Vinnie."

"What about him?"

"I've sort of lost him."

Gritch gave a snort of laughter. "Are you shitting me?"

"He vanished this afternoon. I thought you might know if he was snatched again."

"I haven't heard anything, but then I'm not totally in the loop. It's not like I run with the big boys."

"Understood," I said. "Thanks."

"Sure," Gritch said. "For what it's worth, I hope Vinnie figures a way out of this." And he disconnected.

"I don't know where to go from here," I said to Connie. "Lula and I can ride the circuit of Sunflower's properties again, but I don't think Sunflower will take any chances with Vinnie this time. Vinnie will be locked up tight."

"We have to get the money," Connie said.

"There's no way we're going to gather together that much money," I told her. "I can't catch that many skips. And no bank will loan us that much money by tomorrow. I think we should go to the police."

"I might have more bad news," Connie said. "I've been combing through the office finances, trying to locate money, and I think Vinnie was writing bad bonds."

"You mean giving bonds to people who were bad risks?" I asked.

"No. I mean giving bonds to people who don't exist. I found a file in his office for bonds that never went through our system. And when I run a check on the people who were bonded out, I can't find them, or they're dead, or they're seven years old."

"Why would Vinnie do that?" Lula asked.

"I think Vinnie was running the agency in the red, drawing down from Wellington to cover the bogus skips, and then passing the money on to Gritch."

Lula leaned forward. "Say what?"

"Probably, it started out as a way to cover a couple bad gambling decisions and got out of hand," Connie said. "Vinnie was writing bonds on made-up people with made-up crimes. He'd tell Wellington the bonds were forfeited because the bondee didn't show up for court, and Wellington would reimburse Vinnie for his loss. Then Vinnie would give the money to Gritch, who in turn gave it to Sunflower."

"That don't sound legal," Lula said.

"Not even a little," Connie said. "And I'm involved. I'm responsible for end-of-the-month statements. I wasn't paying attention. I was pushing the phantom bonds on to the accountant."

Oh boy.

"We could rob a couple convenience stores," Lula said. "How hard could it be?"

"We'd have to rob a lot of convenience stores to get that kind of money," I told her.

"Hunh," she said. "You got a better idea?"

"Yes. We could rob Sunflower, and use the money to pay him back. We know two collection points. The funeral home and Chopper's apartment."

Lula's eyes went wide open. "The apartment with the alligator?"

"Yes."

"Un-ah, no way. I'm not robbin' no alligator apartment. Count me out."

"I have a plan," I told her.

Lula put her hands over her ears. "I don't want to hear it."

"I want to hear it," Connie said.

"We hit Chopper first. He leaves his apartment in the early evening to manage his mall business. All his drug money will be in his apartment guarded by the alligator. Hard to say how much money he collects every day, but I'm betting it's sizeable."

159

"What about the gator?" Lula asked.

"I'll take care of the gator," I said. "After we rob Chopper, we go to the funeral home. Lula can go in and open the back door for me. I'll slip in and hide until everyone leaves and the funeral home is locked up for the night. Then I'll go upstairs and get the money out of the counting room."

"They won't just leave the money out," Lula said. "It'll be locked up in the safe. You gotta get the money out before they lock it up. We need to get those guys outta the counting room, and I'm good, but I'm not that good. They're not gonna go for my Girl Scout baloney. And I don't think they're gonna go for Connie's drunk bimbo baloney."

"The stink bomb," Connie said. "I'll set off the stink bomb. Everyone will leave, Stephanie can run upstairs, get the money, and get out of the building." Connie looked over at me. "I'll give you a gas mask."

"How will I get out of the building? Everyone will be outside, milling around."

"Go out the back door," Connie said. "I'll make sure it smells bad enough back there that it'll be deserted."

No one made a sound for a couple beats, absorbing the stupidity of what we were about to do.

"Okay then," I finally said. "Let's do it."

"Rendezvous here at seven," Connie said.

I was halfway home when my mom called.

"Your grandmother went to an afternoon viewing," she said, "and I have no way to get her home. Your father is working, and I'm stuck in traffic on Route

160

One. I'm coming home from the mall, and there must be an accident in front of me, because everything's stopped. I was hoping you could pick your grandmother up at the funeral parlor."

"Sure," I said. "I'll get her."

Grandma was waiting on the porch when I parked in front of the funeral home. She was wearing a blue print dress with a cardigan sweater, one white tennis shoe, and her huge black ortho boot. She was standing lopsided from the boot. I jumped out to help her, but she forged ahead without me. Stomp, step, stomp, step, stomp, step. Down the stairs, hanging on to the railing, her black leather purse hooked over her shoulder.

"Look at this," she said, eyeballing the SUV. "You got another new car. This is a beauty. Did Ranger give this one to you?"

"Yes."

"He must have a lot of money."

I had no idea how much money Ranger had, but he wasn't poor. His address was a vacant lot when I first started working with him, and now he lived in a slick apartment in a building he at least partially owned. The origin of the limitless new black cars was a mystery. And that was part of the problem with Ranger. So much of him was a mystery.

I got Grandma buckled into the Mercedes and pulled away.

"How was the viewing?" I asked her.

"I thought they did a nice job making Miriam look good, considering she didn't look that good to begin with. I don't want to talk bad about the dead, but

Miriam wasn't a natural beauty. Poor thing had them warts all over her face. Her son was there. And her nephew. And they had a nice assortment of cookies. Personally, I prefer the night viewings, but sometimes they interfere with my television shows."

"How's your foot?"

"It's okay. I would have got more attention if they put me in a wheelchair, but they said I would have to rent one of those, and I already spent my social security check. Bitsy Kurharchek has some crutches she said I could borrow, and I might use them for tomorrow night. It's gonna be a big night. Burt Pickeral finally died. He was old as dirt, but he was a royal magoo in the Elks lodge. All the Elks will be there, and all the Pickerals."

"Do you know the Pickerals?"

"I know some of them."

"Do you know Lenny?"

"No, but the name rings a bell. He might be Ralph's boy. There's a mess of Pickerals."

I stopped for a light, pulled the Pickeral file out of my bag, and showed Grandma my file photo of Lenny Pickeral, the toilet paper bandit.

"He looks familiar," Grandma said, "but then all them Pickerals sort of look alike. What's he done?"

"Petty theft."

"That's not so interesting, but I'll keep my eye open for him anyway," Grandma said.

I pulled into the driveway at my parents' house and made sure Grandma got through the front door.

★　★　★

A while back, Morelli's Aunt Rose died and left him her house. It's a two-story row house with basically the same floor plan as my parents' house. Living room, dining room, kitchen on the ground floor. Plus, Morelli added a half bath. Three small bedrooms and bath on the second floor. Morelli has slowly been working at making the house his own, but some of Rose remains, and I think that's nice. Morelli lives there with his big, shaggy, orange dog, Bob, and truth is, Morelli has become surprisingly domesticated . . . although the domestication doesn't seem to extend to the bedroom.

It's a short drive from my parents' house to my apartment if you go straight to Hamilton and turn right. I chose to weave around a couple blocks, cross Chambers, and drive past Morelli's house. I prefer not to think too hard about why I was doing this. I suppose I miss Morelli. Or maybe I wanted to make sure he wasn't having a party without me. No matter the reason, I found myself slowly driving by, looking at the house, feeling some desire to go inside. The green SUV was parked at the curb. Morelli was home. I continued to creep down the street, and the decision to stop or not was settled by momentum. Morelli's house was behind me. Probably not a good time to visit anyway, since I'd have to explain why Ranger gave me a new Mercedes SUV as an indefinite loaner.

The parking lot to my apartment building was almost full when I pulled in. It was approaching dinner time and the seniors and hard-working couples living here were watching sitcom reruns and cooking pasta. I parked in a far corner, where hopefully no one would ding my car, and I jogged into the building, up the stairs, and down the hall. Rex was on his wheel when I swept into the kitchen. He stopped running and looked at me with his whiskers whirring and his black eyes shiny bright. I gave him a piece of cheese, and he rushed into his soup can to eat it. So much for pet interaction.

I made myself a peanut butter and olive sandwich and washed it down with my last beer. I wasn't sure if olives were fruit or vegetable, but they were green, and they were as close as I was going to get to a salad. I wanted to look normal, so I didn't change into the all-black commando deal. I was wearing jeans and a red T-shirt and sneakers, and I thought that was okay. I had time to kill, so I spruced up my eyeliner and added more mascara. I arranged the lipsticks in my junk make-up drawer, and I brushed my teeth. I sprawled on my bed to think, and woke up with a start at twenty minutes to seven.

I grabbed my shoulder bag and did a fast inventory. My stun gun was registering low battery. No point taking it with me. Pepper spray was empty. Throw it away. That left my gun and Pip's bottle. I spun the barrel on the gun. Two bullets. Better than none, right? I didn't want to use my gun anyway. Still, I should make a note to buy more bullets.

I shrugged into a hooded sweatshirt, locked my apartment, and ran to the car. I stopped at Cluck-in-a-Bucket on my way to the office and got two giant-size buckets of extra crispy chicken. Hold the coleslaw and biscuits.

Connie and Lula were already milling around on the sidewalk when I arrived. Lula was holding the box of stink bombs, and Connie had the rocket launcher and two tote bags. I parked behind Connie's Camry and realized I was going to have to make a car decision. If we took the Mercedes, I'd have RangeMan backing me up, but I'd also have witnesses to the whole ridiculous scheme. Push for the Camry, I thought. Best not to have witnesses. I got out with my chicken buckets and beeped the SUV locked.

CHAPTER
SEVENTEEN

Lula perked up at the sight of the chicken. "That smells like extra crispy," she said. "It's my favorite."

"I bought it for Mr Jingles," I told her. "We're going to use it to lure him away from the money."

"Mr Jingles won't mind one less piece," Lula said.

"You're the one who's going to be leading him away with the chicken," I told her. "You don't want to smell like extra crispy."

"In that case, you got a point," Lula said. "I'll pass on the chicken."

"I think we should take the Camry," I said to Connie. "It's the least memorable of the cars."

"I agree," Connie said.

We put all the equipment in the back seat with me, and Connie headed for Chopper's apartment. She drove down Cotter Street, pausing in front of the plumbing supply warehouse. Lights were off. No cars parked in front. Locked up for the night. We looked up at Chopper's windows. No sign of activity. Connie drove around the block and turned into the alley. She sat at idle behind Chopper's apartment, and we all took a couple deep breaths. I stuck my gun in my jeans, and I took one of Connie's tote bags.

"Here's what I think we should do," I said. "Connie will stay in the car for a fast getaway, and Lula and I will go into the apartment. I gather up the money, and Lula keeps Mr Jingles busy with the chicken. Simple, right?"

"Yeah, as long as Mr Jingles likes extra crispy," Lula said.

Lula and I got out of the Camry and scurried across the yard and up the stairs. I found the key, opened the door, and stuck my head in.

"Hello?" I called.

No answer. Also no sound of alligator yawning, alligator running, or alligator sniffing out food.

I crept in and looked around. No stacks of money sitting out on the kitchen counter, dining table, end table. And still no sign of alligator, although the apartment smelled gamey. I walked farther into the apartment and there he was . . . over six feet of alligator behind the couch that sat in the middle of the room. His eyes were open, and he was looking at me.

"G-g-g-gator," I whispered to Lula.

"I see him," Lula said. "Where you want to go first? You want me to get him to the side of the room so you can look in the bedroom?"

"Yeah, that would be good."

"Fetch," Lula said. And she threw a piece of chicken across the room. It hit the wall and fell to the floor, leaving a big grease splotch on the wall.

Mr Jingles swiveled his head toward the chicken but didn't move.

"What the heck kind of gator is this?" Lula said. "This here's Cluck-in-a-Bucket chicken. You don't let Cluck-in-a-Bucket chicken hit the floor and lay there. This here's extra crispy."

"Throw one closer."

She threw a piece right at him. It hit him in the head and bounced off. Snap, he ate it.

"Did you see that?" Lula said. "He didn't even taste that chicken. What's with that?"

"Drop one a couple feet over."

"You bet," Lula said. "Here you go, big guy. Here's a wing."

The gator moved his body in slow motion, making a right turn, and then he lunged and *snap*. Goodbye, wing.

"Whoa," Lula said. "I don't like the way he can do that lunge thing. That's like the death lunge."

She threw a leg close to the wall, and Mr Jingles scrabbled after it, moving faster, catching on to the game.

"Hurry up and go around the other side of the couch," Lula said to me. "Good thing we got two buckets of chicken. Mr Jingles isn't exactly a dainty eater."

I ran around the couch, keeping my eyes on Mr Jingles. I scooted into the bedroom and shut the door. No stacks of money out in the open here, either. I went through the dresser, the closet, looked under the bed. Nothing. I've seen drug money collected, and it's almost always in a backpack or a gym bag. I looked in the bathroom. Very bare-bones. No drug money. I

168

carefully opened the door and looked out. Mr Jingles was stalking Lula around the couch. Lula was throwing chicken everywhere, and Mr Jingles would snap it up and come back at Lula.

"I'm running outta chicken," Lula yelled. "What the heck am I supposed to do when I run outta chicken?"

"How much chicken do you have left?"

"Four pieces."

"Try to get him back to the other side of the room so I can get out of the bedroom."

"Okay, but hurry up. I don't like the way he's lookin' at me."

Lula threw a thigh across the room. Mr Jingles gave the chunk of chicken a cursory glance and turned his attention back to Lula.

"Uh-oh," Lula said. "I think he's figured out the chicken comes from the bucket."

"Then throw the bucket across the room. Just don't leave me trapped here."

Lula whistled. "Here, boy. Nice Mr Jingles. Go get the bucket." Lula wound up to throw the bucket, and Mr Jingles lunged at her. "Yow!" Lula said, staggering back, falling over the ottoman.

The chicken bucket flew out of her hand, hit the open door, and bounced off onto the porch. Mr Jingles rushed after the bucket, ate the bucket, ate the remaining three pieces, and lumbered down the stairs.

I was out of the bedroom and Lula was up off the floor, and we were mouths-open, watching Mr Jingles step onto the cement pad at the bottom of the stairs and amble across the yard to the Camry. Connie frantically powered the window up and looked at us with her what-the-fuck expression. Mr Jingles nosed the Camry, gave Connie the eye, and waddled off down the alley.

"This ain't good," Lula said. "Chopper gonna be mad you let his alligator loose."

"I'm not worried about Chopper. I'm worried about the dogs and cats and kids in the neighborhood."

"Maybe we should call the alligator police," Lula said.

Someone screamed half a block away.

"Okay, I guess we don't have to call the police," Lula said. "And it looks like Connie's on the phone. I don't imagine she's ordering pizza. We should finish up here."

"I can't find the money."

"Maybe Chopper took it with him."

"That's not the pattern."

We looked around the room.

"Not a lot of places to hide a big bag of money," Lula said.

"The couch," I said to her. "Mr Jingles was always by the couch."

We pulled the cushions off. No money.

"Help me lift it," I said to Lula.

We picked the couch up and looked under. Large duffle bag, zippered shut. Chopper had carved out part of the couch. I snagged the bag and looked inside. Lots of money.

A car horn beeped from the alley. Connie was telling us to get out of the apartment.

"We're done here," I said to Lula. "Let's go."

"Yeah," she said. "I hear a siren. I bet it's the alligator police."

I ran to the door, flew down the stairs, and jumped into the back of the Camry with Lula a hair behind me. Connie drove down the alley, and just before the cross street, we passed Mr Jingles steadily moving along, looking like he knew where he was going.

Connie gave an involuntary shiver. I gnawed on my lower lip. And Lula took a disposable wet paper towel from her purse and wiped chicken grease off her hands.

"So that went well," Lula said.

"We let an alligator loose in the neighborhood!" I told her.

"Yeah, but aside from that, it went well."

"Did you call animal control?" I asked Connie.

"Yes. They should be here any minute." Connie turned onto Cotter. "How much money did we get?"

I pawed through the bag. "Rough estimate would be close to a hundred thousand. Might be more."

"That's a lot of money," Lula said, "but it's not enough."

"There should be a lot more at the funeral home," Connie said. "I'm guessing that's a major collection point."

I leaned forward and put my head between my knees. I wasn't cut out for this. My mother was right. I needed a nice, boring job at the personal products factory. Maybe I should stop being a bounty hunter and marry Morelli. Of course, Morelli wasn't sure he wanted to marry me right now, but I might be able to change his mind. I could go over to his house wearing my red thong and a good attitude and catch him at a weak moment. Then we'd get married immediately before he changed his mind. And knowing Morelli, I'd get pregnant. And it would be a boy.

"I'm not naming him Joseph," I said. "It's too confusing."

"Who?" Lula said.

"Did I just say that out loud?" I asked her.

"Yeah. What the heck were you talkin' about?"

"It's not important."

"I tell you what's important," Lula said. "Fried chicken. I can't get it outta my head ever since I had to watch Mr Jingles eat all that extra crispy. I think we need to stop at Cluck-in-a-Bucket on the way across town."

"We'll stop on the way home," Connie said. "If we don't do the funeral home right away, I'm going to lose my nerve."

"Yeah, I hear you," Lula said, "but that's the wrong attitude. That's delayin' pleasure, and you do that, and you might never get to the pleasure. Like, what if we get shot or arrested or something and then we can't get to Cluck-in-a-Bucket? You see what I'm sayin'? Like, we might be dead and then there'd be no extra crispy ever again. And all because we decided to go rob some crazy drug dealer before goin' to Cluck-in-a-Bucket."

I had my head back between my knees. I didn't want to die or go to jail. And if I got out of this unscathed, I was going straight to RangeMan. I was going to strip Ranger naked and squeeze every last drop of pleasure out of him. Then I'd marry Morelli. Somewhere deep

172

in my panic-fogged mind, I suspected this was faulty reasoning, but I couldn't get a grip on it, what with all the nausea and inability to breathe properly.

"Are you okay?" Connie said to me. "I can't see you in my mirror. Where are you?"

"Tying my shoe."

"We're almost there. Let's review the plan one last time. I'll drive by the front so we can scope things out and drop Lula off. Then I'll drive by the back and park someplace close. Lula will open the back door and give Stephanie cover while Stephanie finds a place to hide. Then Stephanie will put the gas mask on and wait for my all-clear signal."

"How are we getting the stink bomb in the funeral home with all the windows barred?" Lula wanted to know.

"I have three jars of liquid stink," Connie told Lula. "You're going to have to dump them at strategic locations, and then get out before you throw up."

"Sure. I could do that," Lula said.

"You're going to need to sneak upstairs and dump a jar in front of the counting room," Connie said. "Then dump another at the back door and another in the front of the funeral home. Try not to get it on top of the deceased. I have the rocket launcher as backup, but it's a last resort. We don't want Sunflower to think he's being attacked."

The funeral home looked business-as-usual when Connie rolled by. A few men in dark suits stood to the side of the front door. They were smoking and quietly talking. Several cars were parked at the curb. We dropped Lula off at the corner, and I handed her the small tote bag with the three jars.

"Good luck," I said. "I'll be waiting at the back door for you."

Lula walked down the sidewalk, and Connie turned into the alley and parked behind the mortuary's Dumpster. Sunflower's Ferrari was parked in the small lot, and a Dodge Minivan was parked next to the Ferrari. I took the large tote bag containing a respirator mask, and I walked to the back door and stood to one side. I had some butterflies in my stomach, but I was focusing now. Get the job done, I thought. Steal the money. Give it back. Save Vinnie's miserable butt. Do some food shopping. I was making a list. Milk, bread, orange juice, beer, an apple for Rex, toilet paper, bullets.

The back door to the funeral home creaked open and Lula looked out at me. "Show time," she said. "Looks to me like the best place to hide is the cellar. You could stand on the stairs. Just make sure you put the mask on, 'cause I'm gonna dump stink there."

Lula stood in the middle of the hall, shielding me from sight, and I scooted through the cellar door and held tight two steps down. Lula closed the door, and I was in total blackness.

Good thing I'm not claustrophobic, I thought. Or afraid of the dark. Okay, maybe I was a little claustrophobic and afraid of the dark, but I could deal. That's what separates the men from the girls, right? The girls can deal.

174

I heard muffled conversation through the door. It was flowing down the hall from the public viewing room. I put the mask on and adjusted the straps. Hard to believe I would need a mask for a stink bomb. I mean, how bad could it be? I had my cell phone in hand, waiting for Connie's call. I checked the time by the phone. It was going on five minutes. Conversation turned loud, and people were in the hall, jostling against the cellar door, gagging and shrieking, trying to get out the back door as fast as possible. A few more minutes passed and my phone buzzed with a text message from Connie.

GO!

I opened the cellar door to an empty hall. Don't fail me now, I said to my feet, and I ran the short distance to the stairs and took them two at a time. I ran into the counting room and almost fainted. The table was filled with money. It was all bundled in stacks and secured with rubber bands. More money than I'd ever seen. The tote bag was huge, but it couldn't hold all of the money. A large duffel bag had been tossed to the floor not far from the table. I stuffed it full of the remaining bundles and still had a couple left. I stuffed them into my bra and my pants, and I hurled myself down the stairs, hanging on to the tote and the duffel. I raced down the short hall and slid to a stop at the door. I said a short prayer, opened the door, and found Connie standing there, wearing a mask.

Connie grabbed my arm and yanked me forward. "Run," she said. "There's a fire truck out front and another at the corner. And some Sunflower goon just arrived in a full contamination suit."

Lula was in the car with the motor running. We dove in, and Lula took off.

CHAPTER
EIGHTEEN

I ripped the mask off my face and took a deep breath. "Whoa," I said. "What the heck is that smell?"

"It's you," Connie said. "You've absorbed stink."

"It's horrible! I smell like vomit and really bad cheese."

"Yeah," Connie said. "This was a good batch."

Lula rolled the windows down. "My eyes are watering. I'm losing my appetite for chicken. Are both those bags full of money?"

"Yep." I took money out of my pants and my bra and handed it over to Connie. "I have no idea how much money is here. I didn't take the time to look. I just stuffed everything in the bags and ran. I got there at a good time. The safe was open but empty. They were either getting ready to put the money away or move it."

"I can't believe we did this," Lula said. "This was totally the shit. This was the bomb. And it don't even look like we're being followed."

Connie and I turned and looked to make sure.

"I think we pulled it off," Connie said.

And she giggled. And then Lula and I giggled. This was pretty weird, because we're not necessarily gigglers, but men spit and scratch their nuts and do high-five hand slaps when they get away with stupid shit . . . and women giggle. I'm not sure which is worse, but I'm glad I'm not inclined to scratch myself in private places in public.

"We're good," Lula said. "How many bitches could steal all this money and not get caught? I'm telling you, I'm talking about a new career. We could be the Three Mouseketeers."

"I think you mean Musketeers," I said to Lula.

"Whatever. We could give ourselves a cool name, and we could do heists and capers. Only thing is, next time we gotta call a cab for Stephanie, so she doesn't smell up the car. I'm glad we're not in my Firebird."

"I can't help it," I said. "I was stuck in the building. For that matter, you don't smell like roses, either."

"Me?" Lula said. "Are you telling me I stink?"

"Yeah."

Connie cut her eyes to Lula. "She's right. You reek."

"I might have spilled some on my shoe," Lula said. "You just filled up old olive bottles, and they didn't pour perfect. Next time, you want to invest in a beaker or something with a spout."

"I don't want to hear about next time," I said. "I'm retiring from a life of crime."

"But we're so good," Lula said. "I bet we made ourselves millionaires."

"Only for half a day. Tomorrow, the money goes back to Sunflower," I told her.

"Oh yeah, I forgot for a minute," Lula said. "Are we sure we want to do that? I could buy a lot of shoes that don't smell bad with that money."

There was silence while the thought hung in the car. Keeping the money had a lot of appeal. If we had the money, we wouldn't actually need Vinnie or the bonds office. Unfortunately, there was Grandma Plum and Aunt Mim to consider. Not to mention the nagging need to do the right thing, and the fear that God would get me if I didn't.

Lula pulled into the Cluck-in-a-Bucket drive-through, and we got a large tub of extra crispy, triple coleslaw, and biscuits.

"Now where to?" Lula wanted to know.

"To the office," Connie said. "We need to count the money. Park the car in the back."

There was an alley behind the office with parking for a couple cars. The back door led to the storeroom, and beyond the storeroom were banks of file cabinets. You could sneak in through the back door and not be seen, unless, of course, you walked through the front office, where Connie held court. Vinnie parked in the back because Vinnie was always hiding out from someone. Vinnie didn't pay his bills on time. He messed around with married women. And he dated barnyard animals.

Lula parked Connie's car, and we hauled the chicken and money and assorted weapons inside and locked the back door.

"Take it all into Vinnie's inner office," Connie said. "There aren't any windows in there."

I cleared Vinnie's desk and dumped the money out.

"We need a system," Connie said, helping herself to an extra crispy mystery piece of chicken. "First, let's divide the money by amount. All the twenties over there in the corner. All the hundreds here by the desk. Just pile it up on the floor. Then we'll use elastic bands to bundle them, so all the bundles are worth the same amount of money."

Two hours later, the bucket of extra crispy was empty and we had all the money bundled, stacked, and counted.

"The latest demand was for one million three," Connie said. "We have a little over one million two."

"Ordinarily, Sunflower might be willing to make a deal," Lula said, "but he just got robbed, and he's probably in a bad mood now."

"I'll call him tomorrow," Connie said. "I can't imagine him not taking one million two."

I looked at the pile of money heaped on Vinnie's desk. "What are we going to do with this until tomorrow? It's not going to fit in Vinnie's safe."

"We'll put the stacks of high-denomination bills in the safe," Connie said. "The rest can get hidden from view under his desk. I'll lock Vinnie's office door and set the alarm when we leave."

I stopped at the all-night supermarket on the way home and got everything on my list but bullets. I parked in the lot behind my apartment building, grabbed the grocery bags from the back seat, turned, and bumped into a rock-solid guy. Morelli.

"Jeez!" I said. "You scared the heck out of me. Don't sneak up on me like that."

"I didn't sneak. You parked next to me and didn't even notice."

"I have a lot on my mind."

"Want to share it?"

I paused for a minute, hugging the bags to me, debating. "No," I said. "I can't."

"You smell really bad," Morelli said. "Like a stink bomb."

"That's ridiculous."

"Where were you tonight?"

"I went out for dinner with Lula and Connie."

"Someone set a stink bomb off in Bobby Sunflower's funeral home," Morelli said.

"And?"

"The only one I know who can build a stink bomb of that magnitude is Connie. She was in my graduating class in high school, and she was famous."

"Why would Connie set off a stink bomb in Sunflower's funeral home?"

"You tell me."

Our eyes locked for a moment before I turned away. "Don't know," I said.

Morelli took the bags from me and walked me to the building. "That's a fib."

"It's my story," I said, "and I'm sticking to it."

He held the door for me and followed me through the foyer and into the elevator.

"This could be a romantic moment if you smelled better," he said.

I found it hard to believe a little stink would deter Morelli's libido. Since becoming a bounty hunter, I've smelled like dog poop, garbage, blown-up funeral home, and monkey. It's hard to believe stink bomb was

181

any worse. The elevator doors opened, and Morelli tagged behind me.

"Here's what's confusing me," he said. "I know Connie's stink bombs pretty well, and you're definitely smelling like a stink bomb, but there's also a hint of fried chicken."

"Cluck-in-a-Bucket," I said. "Extra crispy."

Morelli stopped in the middle of my hall. "Omigod. You're the one who turned Mr Jingles loose."

I plugged the key into my lock and opened the door. "It wasn't me, I swear."

Morelli set the bags on my counter and helped himself to a beer. "Lula?"

"I'm not saying. Was anyone hurt? Did any dogs or cats get eaten?"

Morelli chugged some beer. "Negative. Mr Jingles got caught without incident. Animal control went to serve Chopper with a ticket, and they said his door was open and there were grease stains all over his apartment and it smelled like fried chicken and alligator."

"Go figure," I said.

He lounged against the counter. "I don't suppose I could persuade you to take a shower."

"No persuading necessary. I can't stand myself. I'm going to take a shower and throw my clothes away. It's what might happen after the shower that would be a hard sell."

"My specialty," Morelli said. "I might even start the hard sell while you're in the shower."

"I thought you wanted to date other women."

182

"I didn't want to date other women. We decided in the heat of battle that we were no longer exclusively attached."

"And I could date other men."

Morelli was starting to look annoyed. "Have you been dating other men?"

"Maybe."

"As long as it isn't Ranger," Morelli said.

"I don't think Ranger dates."

The idea of Ranger dating was pretty strange. I've seen him in bars, stalking skips. And I've had dinner with him on occasion, but I couldn't imagine him calling a woman up for a date. I suspected he had a small list of non-threatening, cooperative women who he visited late at night when the mood struck.

"Whatever it is Ranger does, I don't want him doing it with you," Morelli said. "He's a nut. And he's dangerous."

"He's mellow now," I told Morelli. "He's a businessman."

Morelli looked out at the black Mercedes. "Do you know where he gets these cars?"

"No. Do you?"

"No, but I doubt it's a legal source."

I wasn't even sure it was a human source. It was like the cars were beamed in from space.

"Are we fighting?" I asked Morelli.

"No. We're discussing."

"Are you sure?"

"Am I yelling?" Morelli asked. "Is my face purple? Are the cords in my neck standing out? Am I waving my arms around?"

"No."

"Then we're not fighting."

I kicked my shoes off in the kitchen and peeled my socks off. "Were you working tonight?"

"No."

"Then how do you know about Mr Jingles and the funeral home?"

"I went out to get a pizza and ran into Eddie coming off his shift. He got to help wrangle Mr Jingles into the animal control van."

Eddie Gazarra is a uniformed cop who's married to my cousin Shirley-the-Whiner. He's a nice guy with a white-blond buzz cut and a big mouth.

I unzipped my jeans. "I need to get out of these contaminated clothes. I don't want them in my bedroom. Are you going to stand here and watch me get undressed?"

His brown eyes almost completely dilated to black. "Yeah," he said. "I'm going to watch you get undressed. And I'm going to watch you take a shower. And then I'm personally going to towel you down."

Oh boy. Oh boy!

I dropped my jeans, stepped out of them, and Morelli's phone rang. Morelli didn't take his eyes off me. He didn't answer his phone. He didn't check the readout. The phone kept ringing.

"Your phone," I said.

"It'll stop."

There was a moment's pause while the phone disconnected. And then the phone buzzed with a text message and buzzed a second time.

184

"You might as well read it," I said. "It's not going away."

Morelli glanced at his phone. "I've got a text message from dispatch and a text message from my boss." He punched a number in and waited.

"Yeah?" Morelli said when the connection opened.

His attention moved from me to a spot on the floor. He listened for a full minute before raising his head and looking back at me.

"I'm on it," he said. And he slid his phone into his pocket.

"Well?" I asked.

"I have to go. Two guys in suits and ties were just found facedown in the Regal Diner parking lot. They were behind the Dumpster in an area reserved for employees. Hands tied. Single bullet in the back of the head."

"Execution."

"Yeah."

"Have they been ID'd?"

"Not that I can tell you. Ranger monitors all our communication. I'm sure you can get it from him. All I can say is that they weren't from the neighborhood."

"Boy, this is too bad," I said. "I was planning on being incredibly sexy after I got clean."

"That's rotten," Morelli said. "You were the one who told me to take the message." He took a step toward me and pulled back. "I'd kiss you, but you smell like my gym bag."

I locked the door when Morelli left, removed the rest of my clothes, and stuffed them into a black plastic garbage bag. I sprayed my sneakers with deodorizer and hoped for the best. I took a shower and washed my hair twice. I got dressed in a T-shirt and boxer shorts and called Ranger.

"Babe," he said.

"Who were the two suits dumped behind Regal Diner tonight?"

"Victor Kulik and Walter Dunne. A couple lawyers who work in mergers and acquisitions for a venture capital company. It's the same company that bought the bail bonds agency from Harry. Wellington."

"Thanks."

"You stole money from Chopper and Sunflower so you could give it back to Sunflower and bail Vinnie out, didn't you?"

"Who me?"

"Anyone else would have just killed the alligator," Ranger said.

"How do you know?"

"I know everything."

"And you're modest."

"No," Ranger said. "I'm not modest."

And he disconnected.

CHAPTER
NINETEEN

Most mornings, I'm rushed and my refrigerator is empty and I take breakfast where I find it. This morning, I was flush with food from my supermarket stop, so I had orange juice, coffee, and a bowl of Rice Krispies for breakfast. I gave Rex a chunk of apple, some hamster crunchies, and fresh water. I checked my e-mail. I lined my eyes with a very thin line of smoky black and brushed on a smidgen of mascara. My sneakers still smelled a little, but, fortunately, they were far from my nose.

I'd taken the lucky bottle out of my bag last night, and I had it sitting on my kitchen counter. If I was to be perfectly honest, it wasn't all that great a bottle. And I wasn't sure why Uncle Pip left it to me. I liked Uncle Pip, but I wasn't any closer to him than a lot of other relatives. Why he singled me out to have his lucky bottle was a mystery. I held the bottle to the light, but I couldn't see inside. I thought I heard something when I shook the bottle, but it was very faint. Hard to tell if it was bringing me luck. I didn't get trampled by stampeding cows, eaten by an alligator, or shot while robbing a funeral home, so maybe the bottle was working.

I put my dishes in the sink, told Rex to be a good hamster, and I set off for my parents' house with my garbage bag of stink-bomb clothes. There are washers and dryers in the basement of my building, but I'm pretty sure trolls live there.

My grandmother was sitting with her foot up on a kitchen chair when I walked in.

"How's the foot?" I asked.

"It's a pain in the keister. I'm tired of hearing clomp, clomp, clomp. And it takes me a half hour to go up the stairs. And it hurts if I walk on it too much, so I'm sitting around going nuts. I'm not used to sitting around." She leaned forward and wrinkled her nose. "Holy cow, who let one go? What's that smell?"

I held up the garbage bag. "My clothes were in the wrong place at the wrong time. They need washing."

"Leave them on the back porch," my mother said. "I'll do them later."

"We got coffee cake," Grandma said to me. "And there's some breakfast sausages in the refrigerator."

"Thanks," I said, "but I just ate breakfast."

My mother and grandmother looked at me.

"You ate breakfast?" my mother asked. "I thought you broke up with Joseph."

Morelli isn't Martha Stewart, but it's a known fact he's more organized than I am. Morelli almost always has food in his house. When we're a couple, and I spend the night, I eat breakfast at his little wooden kitchen table. Sometimes it's leftover pizza and sometimes it's a frozen toaster waffle. And Morelli is always the one to start coffee brewing, because Morelli is always the first one up. His kitchen is almost identical to my mom's, but it feels entirely different. He's refinished the wood floor and put in new cabinets. The lighting is pleasant, and the counters are for the most part uncluttered in Morelli's house. My mom's kitchen hasn't changed much since I was a kid. Some new appliances, and new curtains on the back window. The floor is vinyl tile. The counters are Formica. The cabinets are maple. And the kitchen smells like coffee, apple pie, and bacon even when my mother isn't cooking.

"I ate breakfast at home," I said.

"Are you pregnant?" Grandma asked. "Sometimes women do strange things when they're pregnant."

"I'm not pregnant! I went shopping and got orange juice and Rice Krispies, and I ate breakfast at home. Jeez. It's not like I never eat at home."

"You only got one pot," Grandma said.

"I had more pots, but they got wrecked when my stove caught fire." I put the garbage bag on the back porch and took a seat at the table with Grandma. "Maybe just one piece of coffee cake," I said.

Two pieces of cake and two cups of coffee later, I pushed back and stood.

"I need Lula to help me decorate this big black boot," Grandma said. "I think it needs some of that glitter, or some rhinestones. Lula has a real flare for fashion."

Ten minutes later, I was looking for a parking place in front of the bonds office. Cars were lined up on the curb. Some were double-parked. Some were angled in nose first. Soccer mom vans, junkers, tricked-out Escalades, Civics, and F150s. Mooner's RV was parked in front of the bookstore. A crowd of people was milling around on the sidewalk. Hard to tell what was going on from the road. And then I saw the sign as I drove past. SIDEWALK SALE.

I parked half a block away and walked back to where Lula was directing pedestrian traffic.

"You want genuine first-class handcuffs, you just go to table number three," she called out. "You could have a lot of fun with these handcuffs. They fit just right around a bedpost. Handguns are table six. We got a nice selection. Kitchen appliances and jewelry's inside."

"What's going on?" I asked her.

"Sale," Lula said. "Sunflower wouldn't negotiate, so we're sellin' everything. You want a lawnmower? It's gonna go cheap."

"I haven't got a lawn."

"Oh yeah, I forgot."

"Where's Connie?"

"Inside. She's doing credit card sales. I'm strictly cash out here."

Lula was dressed in four-inch black micro-fiber heels decorated with multicolored glitter, a short purple Spandex skirt, a gold metallic tank top, and she was wearing a Tavor Assault Rifle as an accessory.

"What's with the gun?" I asked her.

"It's in case some of these people get unruly."

A big bald guy in a wife-beater shirt and cami cargo pants came up to Lula.

"Hey, Lula," he said.

"My man," Lula said to him.

"I need a gun," he said to Lula. "Are these legal?"

"Do you want them to be?" Lula asked.

"No. Shit, what would I want with a legal gun?"

"Don't know," Lula said, "but these suckers are whatever the hell you want them to be. Cash only."

I snaked my way through the crowd to Connie. "What's going on?" I asked her.

Connie stepped back, away from a woman checking out a waffle iron. "Sunflower won't deal. He wants all the money, so Lula and I came up with the idea for the sidewalk sale. This stuff was all taken in exchange for bond and never reclaimed. It was just taking up space in the back room, so we figured we'd sell it."

"Lula's selling weapons out there!"

"That's great," Connie said. "They're a high-ticket item."

"I think it's illegal to sell guns like this."

Connie craned her neck and looked through the front window at Lula. "It's okay," Connie said. "That guy's a cop."

"How much are these dishes with the roses on them?" a woman wanted to know.

"Twenty dollars," Connie said.

A second woman elbowed in. "Wait a minute. Those are my dishes. I gave them to you so my nephew could get out of jail."

Connie looked at the sticker on the bottom of a plate. "We've had these dishes for a year and a half."

"It don't matter. They're mine."

"Where's your nephew?" Connie asked.

"Tennessee."

The first woman handed Connie a twenty and started stacking up her dishes.

"Police!" the second woman yelled. "There's a robbery going on here."

Lula ran in with her gun. "Did someone say robbery?"

"It was a misunderstanding," I told Lula. "Don't shoot anyone."

"It was no misunderstanding," the second woman said. "Those are my dishes. This old lady here was gonna walk out with them."

"Old? Excuse me," the first woman said. "You're not exactly a spring chicken. And these are my dishes. I saw them first."

They both had hold of a plate, and they were nose to nose, eyes narrowed.

Mooner strolled over with a plate of brownies. "Ladies, have a bite of a Moon Man brownie. We're selling them out front, but these are free samples. I made these brownies in my very own test kitchen in the Love Bus."

We all took a time-out so the ladies and Lula could have a brownie.

"These are real good brownies," Lula said. "These are doughnut-quality brownies."

"I changed my mind," woman number one said. "I don't want the dishes. I'm buying brownies."

"I don't want the dishes, either," woman number two said. "I never liked them anyway."

192

Lula took a second brownie and went back to patrol the sidewalk.

"If she keeps eating brownies, we're going to have to take her keys away," Connie said. "I don't know exactly what's in Mooner's brownies, but my guess is they're at least sixty percent controlled substance."

"I'm surprised Sunflower wouldn't take what you offered for Vinnie."

"He was in a vicious mood. He said we were lucky he was holding at a million three. And we have until nine o'clock tomorrow morning."

"Did you discuss how the trade-off was going to work?"

"No. He didn't want to talk. He was really cranky. He gave me his demand and hung up on me."

"Guess things aren't going good in Sunflower Land."

Lula pushed her way back to us.

"Watch out. Comin' through. Outta my way," she was saying. "I just sold all our guns," she said to Connie. "We got any more?"

"No, that was it," Connie said. "I saved the good stuff for our personal use. I have them locked down in the back room."

"Too bad," Lula said. "There's a couple guys buying up everything. I sold them a case of cuffs Vinnie got at that fire sale. And they bought the box of dynamite that got wet when the roof leaked in January."

"Local guys?"

"Nope. They were from Idaho. They said they were part of some militia, here on a recruiting drive."

"Uh-oh," Connie said, looking past me. "Morelli's at the door, and he doesn't look happy."

"Probably, he wanted some of them guns," Lula said. "That's what happens when you don't get here early. You miss out on all the best stuff."

Morelli made his way back to us and clamped a hand around my wrist. "We need to talk."

"Howdy," Lula said. "You're lookin' fine today, Officer Morelli."

Morelli made a half-hearted attempt not to smile. "You're going to have to cut her off from the brownies," he said to Connie.

"I'd chain her to the streetlight, but she sold all my handcuffs," Connie said.

Morelli pulled me past the file cabinets to the back door.

"What the hell's going on?" he said. "I was driving by on my way to the station, and I saw a couple neo-Nazis loading guns into the back of their van."

"They were neo-Nazis?"

"And there's a line halfway down the block to buy Mooner's brownies. I don't suppose you checked the ingredients?"

"Chocolate, eggs, flour . . ." I said.

"There's not a person in that line who'll be able to pass a drug test."

He leaned close to me, nuzzling my neck, his lips brushing my ear. "You smell nice again."

"You, too. You smell like . . . brownie!"

Morelli grinned down at me. "I don't know where he's getting it, but he's got some really good shit in those brownies."

"Are you going to shut him down?"

194

"No. By the time I get back to him, he'll have sold out, and the problem will be solved."

"How'd it go with the dead lawyers?"

"Complete cluster fuck. I didn't get home until four in the morning. I've had four hours of sleep. The feds had to come in and do their thing. The crime-scene truck broke down and was two hours late. It took forever to get the bodies released to the ME. And now I've got extra paperwork."

He looked to the front of the office. "This is a zoo. It's like vultures fighting over a dead cow."

I looked around. "Yeah, getting to be only bones left. It's amazing what Connie's sold in two hours."

"The brownies helped."

"Do you like being a cop?" I asked him.

"Sometimes. Why do you ask?"

"I'm not sure I like being a bounty hunter anymore."

"What would you rather do?"

"That's the problem," I said. "I don't know. I've never had a passion for anything. I went into retail after college because I like to shop, but I didn't especially like my job. And I'm not sure I was good at it. And then I became a bounty hunter because I couldn't get anything else. And I know I'm not the world's best bounty hunter."

"You make a lot of captures," Morelli said.

"Wow, are you being supportive of my job?"

"No. I hate your job, but you're not horrible at it."

"That's the problem. I'm not horrible at it. I want to be wonderful at something."

"I know a few things you're wonderful at."

"Good grief."

Morelli hooked a finger under the shoulder strap on my tank top. "Would you like me to list them?"

"No!"

"Tonight?"

"Maybe tonight," I said.

Morelli leaned into me and kissed me lightly on the lips. "You're such a cupcake."

I supposed that was good, but I wasn't sure. I watched Morelli walk away, and I had a rush of tenderness, and then I got a rush of lust. Morelli was flat-out handsome, and I knew a few of *his* talents, too.

I went back to Connie. She was packing the service for eight in a box while a woman waited. She gave the woman the box and she left, elbowing her way through the crowd.

"I'm going to cut this off at noon," Connie said. "We only have junk left. Nothing that's going to bring any real money."

"Is there anything I can do?"

"Yeah, you can get food. When I shut this down, we'll count everything up. Lula's either going to be passed out or have the munchies real bad by then."

196

CHAPTER
TWENTY

When I returned to the office a little after noon, the tables were gone from the sidewalk and the cars and trucks were also gone. Mooner's RV was still parked in front of the bookstore, but Mooner wasn't in sight. Most likely, he was inside the Love Bus planning out Hobbit Con. I carted the bags of food into the office and set it all out on Connie's desk.

Connie was working with a calculator, adding in money she'd arranged in stacks on the floor. She had a Glock on the desk beside her phone. Lula was asleep on the couch. Lula woke up when she heard the food bags rustling.

"Is that food? God bless whoever brought food. I'm starved."

"I have meatball subs and potato salad and macaroni from Pino's," I told her.

Connie took a sub and kept working, plugging numbers into the calculator.

"How are we doing?" I asked her.

"I think we're going to make it. The guns and the motorcycle helped a lot."

"That whole back room is just about empty," Lula said. "Only thing left is dust bunnies."

I sat back and ate my lunch and watched traffic move past the bonds office. The rhythm on the street was normal again. I imagined the militiamen were on their way back to Idaho with their dynamite, and some woman in the Burg was setting her new service for eight in her china closet.

"That's it," Connie said. "We have a million three for Sunflower and fifty-two dollars left over. I have the fifty-two dollars on my desk. Everything else can get packed. Count it as you go. We want to give Sunflower a million three. No more. No less."

"What are we gonna put it in?" Lula asked.

Connie collected the lunch wrappers and stuffed them into the Pino's bag. "We have a couple duffel bags in the back that were holding guns. We sold the guns, but I kept the bags."

"Do you think Sunflower will recognize his money?" Lula asked.

"No. It's all been rebundled," Connie said to Lula. "So far as we know, we weren't seen at Chopper's, and you were the only one seen at the funeral parlor. I doubt they'd attribute the robberies to you."

"Yeah," Lula said. "Sunflower's one of them chauvinistic underestimators."

Lula and I set to work packing the duffel bags, being careful to count as we packed, and Connie called Sunflower.

"He sounded happier this time," Connie said when she got off the phone. "I think he needs the money."

"Where are we making the switch?" I asked her.

"He wants us to bring the money to the back door of the bar. I told him we wouldn't go inside, so he's going to have his man waiting for us."

"We'll take the Mercedes," I said to Connie. "Ranger monitors all his cars. If anything bad goes down, we'll have Ranger backing us up."

I drove the Mercedes to the parking area behind the bonds office, and Lula and Connie lugged the duffel bags out and put them on the back seat. Connie got in the front passenger seat and set her Uzi on the floor, between her feet. Lula squeezed herself onto the back seat next to the duffel bags filled with money. Lula had her Glock in her purse and a sawed-off shotgun wedged between her legs.

I had my gun with two bullets.

"Vinnie better appreciate this," Lula said. "I'm expecting a raise. And I want a company car. Not just any car, either. I want a good one. And I want one of them tower of treats at Christmas. You know, where you get it in the mail, and it's a stack of boxes with all kinds of shit in 'em."

"I don't want a raise," Connie said. "I want to rescue Vinnie, and then I want to kick his perverted ass all the way from the bonds office to the hospital."

I drove across town and turned up Stark Street. I had my eye on my rearview mirror. No RangeMan tail in view, but I knew Chet was following my blip on his screen. Connie and Lula were silent. We were all in alert mode. I rolled past the bar, took the next cross street for half a block, and turned into the alley.

Three goons were waiting outside the bar's back door. No Vinnie. I crept down the alley and stopped at the bar. Connie powered her window down, and the men stepped forward. Connie poked her Uzi out the window, and the men stopped in their tracks.

"Do you have the money?" one of the men asked.

"Yes," Connie said. "Do you have Vinnie?"

"No. Why would we have Vinnie?"

"You recaptured him."

"Not that I know of," the guy said. "I'm just supposed to get the money from you. You give us the money, and we don't blow up the bail bonds office with all of you in it, including Vinnie."

"I need a moment," Connie said to the men. And she powered her window up.

"What the heck is this?" Lula said. "I'm confused."

Connie looked over at me. "What do you think?"

"I don't think they have him," I said.

Connie gave a curt nod. "That's what I think."

"So who's got him?" Lula asked.

"Don't know," Connie said, "but if we give them the money, they won't blow us up."

Lula opened her door and dumped the money out on the pavement. "I want a receipt," she said.

"I don't got a receipt," the one guy said. "Mr Sunflower didn't give us no receipt. And anyway, we'd have to count it to give you a real receipt."

"Are you sayin' I'm a cheater?" Lula said to him. "Because you better take it back if that's what you meant to say. You be in for a world of hurt if you slander me."

200

"Cripes, woman," the guy said. "I just don't got a receipt. Cut me some slack here."

"Hunh," Lula said, and she slammed her door shut.

"Guess we're done here," I said.

And I drove off.

"That was sort of a letdown," Lula said. "I expected to get Vinnie back. Not that I even want him back, but we gave those guys a lot of money, and seems like we should get something. I need a doughnut. If you turn onto Broad, there's a doughnut place."

"You can't solve all your problems with doughnuts," I said. "If you keep doing that, I'm going to get fat."

"There's four ways to manage stress," Lula said to me. "There's drugs, there's alcohol, there's sex, and there's doughnuts. I go with sex and doughnuts. I tried the other two and it wasn't any good. You being in a dry spell, you might have to rely on doughnuts."

I turned onto Broad, and a block later, I pulled into a Dunkin' Donuts drive-thru. Lula got a bag of doughnuts, and Connie got a bag of doughnuts.

I took a doughnut from Connie's bag. "So what do we think about Vinnie?"

"I think he's dead," Lula said.

"He hasn't turned up," Connie said.

Lula finished off her first doughnut. "He could be in the morgue."

Connie shook her head. "All the cops know Vinnie. He'd get ID'd if he showed up dead."

"Then they must have shot Vinnie full of holes like Swiss cheese and weighted him down with cement boots and thrown him off the bridge into the Delaware.

Or they could have taken him to a butcher shop and chopped him up into little pieces and put him into the meat grinder," Lula said. "I'm gonna eat this jelly doughnut next. I love jelly doughnuts."

"So dead is one possibility," I said. "What else?"

"Somebody else could have snatched him," Lula said. "Somebody other than Bobby Sunflower."

"Why?" Connie asked.

"I guess to get money, like Sunflower. It could be a copycat snatching," Lula said.

"No one's gotten in touch with us," Connie said.

"Hunh," Lula said. "That's problematic."

"There's something else that I always thought was problematic," I said. "If we're assuming someone took Vinnie, how did they know he was in Mooner's RV? Mooner picked Vinnie up at my parents' house. And Mooner said Vinnie never left the RV."

"I see what you're saying," Lula said. "This had to be one of them opportunistic crimes. Like someone decided to rob Mooner's RV when Mooner went into the bakery, and they come across Vinnie and decided on the spur of the moment to take him, and then they killed him and put him in the meat grinder."

"What's with the meat grinder thing?" I asked her.

"I don't know. I guess I'm feeling like a burger for dinner, and I just keep thinking of meat grinders," Lula said.

I drove down Hamilton and was happy to see the Love Bus was still in front of the bookstore. I maneuvered the Mercedes into a space at the curb and cut the engine.

202

"I want to talk to Mooner," I said to Connie and Lula. "The pieces aren't fitting into the puzzle."

Mooner was at the door to the RV before I knocked. "I was hoping you'd come back," he said. "I was wondering if I could plug into your electric. I'm, like, down on my battery, and the Cosmic Alliance doesn't understand no juice."

"Sure," Connie said. "We're all going down the drain anyway. You have to unplug when I leave for the night."

"Understood. And no worries, I got my own extension cord."

"Talk to me about Vinnie disappearing," I said to Mooner. "Walk me through it again."

"Well, like I said, we were groovin'. We were listening to some Dead and gettin' mellow. I was, like, just drivin' around spreading the word. And next thing, I spotted the bakery, so I wheeled the old bus into the lot."

"Stop," I said. "Picture the lot. Was it empty?"

"No. There were, like, two cars. The big car and the little car."

"An SUV and a sportscar."

"Correcto mundo."

"Were the cars occupied?"

"Don't think so, but I can't be sure. I wasn't paying attention. And suppose someone was, like, lying down on the seat taking a nap? I mean, I wouldn't see them, right? So would that count?"

"Yeah."

"Well then, like, dude."

"What was Vinnie doing when you left for the bakery?"

"He was riding shotgun. And I guess he was looking out the window. Except there wasn't anything to see but the parking lot."

"So Vinnie is in the RV in the shotgun seat and you're walking into the bakery. Was anyone in the lot? Maybe going to their car?"

"No. The lot was empty except for me."

"How about the bakery? Were there any customers in the bakery besides you?"

"No. But you know how the bakery has those two glass doors? So, like, suppose there were two people going in and out of those doors at exactly the same time? Would they be in or would they be out? And, like, would that count?"

"Yes, it would count," I told him.

"Then there was someone else, and she was either in or out. Now that I'm thinking about it, she might have been a teensy bit more out. It was her gazongas that were over the line. She had, like, massive gazongas. They'd definitely crossed the midway line before the rest of her."

"She was coming out when you were going in?"

"Yeah," Mooner said.

"Did you watch her cross the lot?"

"No, man. I was caught in the cinnamon roll tractor beam."

"Okay, so what did she look like?" I asked him.

Mooner grinned. "She had real big gazongas."

"We've already established that," I said.

204

"He got a gazonga fixation," Lula said. "What is it with men and gazongas? It's not like women got a nut fixation. It's not like we go around looking for some guy with basketballs hangin' down to his knees."

"Back to the woman," I said. "How old was she?"

"She was about our age."

"Pretty?"

"Yeah. She was, like, porn-star pretty."

"What the heck is porn-star pretty?" Lula wanted to know.

"Like, out there with the gazongas, you know?"

"You say gazongas one more time, and I'm gonna hit you," Lula said.

"Moving on," I said. "What else?"

"She was wearing a lot of eye make-up, and she had big fat shiny lips, and she was in one of those black leather tops with the shoestrings. And it was, like, hardly holding the . . . you-know-whats in."

"She was wearing a bustier," Lula said.

"And she was in a black leather skirt that was, wow, really short. And stilleto heels."

"Yep, that's a porn star all right," Lula said.

I was pretty sure I knew the porn star, and she was only a porn star in her home movies. "What about hair?" I asked.

"Red. Like Lula's, but there was, like, a lot of it, and it was all in waves and curls. Like a red-haired Farrah Fawcett."

"Joyce Barnhardt," I said.

"Yeah," Mooner said.

"You knew it was Joyce?"

"Sure."

"Why didn't you tell me?"

"You didn't ask me if I knew her name," Mooner said.

"Can I hit him now?" Lula wanted to know.

I cut my eyes to her. "You'd hit the brownie maker?"

"Yeah, good point," Lula said.

"At least we know where Vinnie's hiding out," Connie said.

"Yeah, he took off sniffing after Barnhardt," Lula said. "I'm just surprised he's still there. Barnhardt uses 'em up and kicks 'em out."

Joyce Barnhardt is my arch nemesis. I went all through school with Joyce, and she did her best to make my life a misery. In all fairness to Joyce, I wasn't singled out. Joyce made everyone's life a misery. She was a fat kid who spit on other people's food, looked under the stall door in the bathroom, lied, cheated, and bullied. Somewhere in high school, she morphed into a sexual vampire, and eventually she lost weight, bought breasts, inflated her lips, died her hair, and honed her skills as a home wrecker and user to an all-time high. She's had multiple marriages, each more profitable than the previous, and she's currently single and hunting. She drives a flashy Corvette and lives in a large house not far from Vinnie.

"Let's saddle up," I said to Lula.

"You going to get Vinnie?" she asked.

"Yes. I don't know why, but I feel compelled to retrieve him."

"I hear you," Lula said.

206

CHAPTER
TWENTY-ONE

Joyce lived in a house that was a cross between Mount Vernon and Tara from *Gone with the Wind*. Professionally maintained green lawn leading to a monster white colonial with black shutters and a columned entrance. I turned onto Joyce's street and saw that Vinnie was sitting on the curb in front of the house. He was back to wearing only boxer shorts, and he had a two-day beard.

"That's disgustin'," Lula said. "You aren't gonna let him into this nice car, are you? He's probably got Barnhardt cooties all over him. Maybe you should strap him to the roof."

"I haven't got any bungee cords. He's going to have to ride inside."

I stopped and let Vinnie into the Mercedes.

"What took you so long?" he said.

He was in the back seat, and I looked in my rearview mirror and gave him my death stare.

"You got no manners," Lula said to Vinnie. "I'm gonna have to disinfect my eyes with bleach after seeing you in them shorts. Why are you always just wearing shorts whenever we rescue you?"

"I wasn't wearing anything when I got kicked out," Vinnie said. "The neighbors complained, and Joyce threw these shorts out to me. They're not even mine."

"Why didn't you at least call?"

"Hello?" Vinnie said. "Do you see a phone on me?"

"Guess not any of Joyce's neighbors were gonna open the door to a naked man," Lula said.

"Only long enough to send the dog out after me," Vinnie said.

"So why'd Joyce kick you out?" Lula asked.

"She found out I didn't have any money."

A half hour later, I was back at the office and Vinnie was inside, staring down at the electric cord running out to Mooner's RV. "What the hell?"

"He needed juice for the Cosmic Alliance," Lula said. "Are you gonna put clothes on? I'm gettin' nauseous lookin' at your nasty weasel body."

"My clothes are all in the rolling goof house out there. That guy is a nut. Hasn't anyone ever told him Hobbits aren't real?" Vinnie went to his office and looked around. "What happened to my furniture? All I've got in here is my desk and a folding chair."

"We sold it," Connie said.

"Yeah, we sold everything," Lula told him. "We sold all the dishes, guns, grills, and jewelry. We even sold the motorcycle."

"The BMW? Are you shitting me? That was my private motorcycle."

"Not no more," Lula said.

"We needed the money to buy back your debt," I told him. "You're off the hook with Sunflower and Mickey Gritch."

Mooner ambled in. "Hey, amigo," he said to Vinnie. "Welcome back, dude. Long time, no see."

"Yeah, a lot longer than I wanted. Didn't you give anybody my note?"

"You didn't leave a note."

"Of course I left a note," Vinnie said. "It was on the table. I couldn't find any paper, so I wrote it on a napkin."

"Dude, that was your note? I thought the napkin came like that. You know how you get napkins in bars with funny things written on them?"

"You didn't read it?"

"No, dude, I put my pastries on that napkin. That's what napkins are for . . . drinks and pastries."

"At least I'm back in the office," Vinnie said. "A man's office is his castle, right?" He sat in the folding chair and opened his top drawer. "Where's my gun?"

"Sold it," Connie said.

Vinnie closed the drawer and put his hands on his desk. "Where's my phone?"

"Sold that, too," Connie said.

"How am I supposed to work without a phone?"

"You don't work anyway," Lula said. "And now you can't call your bookie, who, by the way, probably isn't talking to you on account of you got no credit."

"Yeah, but you paid everything off, right? How much did it come to?"

"A million three," Connie said.

Vinnie froze, mouth open. "You paid a million three? Where the hell did you get that kind of money?"

"We sold your phone," I said.

"Yeah, and your bike," Lula said.

"That's not nearly adding up to a million three. Where'd you get the rest of the money?"

"I'd rather not say," I told him.

"Stephanie's right," Connie said. "You don't want to know."

"I came in to unplug," Mooner said. "The Alliance wants me to go to the airport to pick up some Hobbits flying in for the big event."

"Okay, so I don't have a phone," Vinnie said. "It's still good to be here. I tell you, I thought I was going to die. They were serious. I don't know what the deal is with Bobby Sunflower, but he was gonzo. And then when the house got bombed, everyone was twice as nuts. I was happy when you rescued me from the rat-trap apartment, but I figured my time was short. I never thought you'd get me off. I knew Sunflower would track me down and blow my brains out. I figured he'd find me in Antarctica if he had to."

"He needed money," I said.

Vinnie opened his middle drawer and rifled through it. "The petty cash is missing."

"And?" Connie said.

"Well spent," Vinnie said. "It's not like I'm not grateful."

"Why did Sunflower need money?" I asked Vinnie.

"Bad investments, I guess."

"Like what?"

210

Vinnie shrugged. "I don't know. I don't even care. I just want to relax and enjoy not having a contract on me. I want to sit here in my office and watch television for a half hour." Vinnie looked around. "Where's my television? Oh crap, don't tell me you sold my television."

"I got two hundred dollars for it," Lula said.

"It was high def!" Vinnie said. "It was a plasma."

"Well, if you want, I can call Bobby Sunflower and tell him I want two hundred dollars back so you can repo your high def, plasma TV," Lula said.

"Nope, that's okay," Vinnie said. "I'm going to sit here and close my eyes and pretend I have a television. I'm calm. I'm happy to be alive. I'm happy to have gotten out of Joyce's house without getting my Johnson cut off." Vinnie opened his eyes and looked over at us. "She's an animal."

"Too much information," Lula said.

Connie went to her desk to answer the phone. "Vinnie," she called. "It's Roger Drager, president of Wellington. He'd like to talk to you."

"What's Wellington?" Lula asked Vinnie.

"It's the venture capital company that owns the agency."

"Oh yeah," Lula said. "Now I remember."

Vinnie went to Connie's desk to take the call.

"Yeah," he said. "Yessir. Yessir. Yessir." And he hung up.

"That was a lot of yessirs," Lula said.

"He wants me to come to his office," Vinnie said. "Now."

"Be good if you put some clothes on," Lula said. "He might not like little Vinnie hangin' out your shorts."

"I'll get them," Mooner said. "They're in the Love Bus."

"What does he want to talk to you about?" Connie asked.

"I don't know," Vinnie said.

"Maybe it's the phantom bonds," Connie said.

Vinnie's eyebrows lifted. "You know about that?"

"We scoured the office, looking for money, and I found the file."

"It started out small. I swear on my mother's grave I meant to pay Wellington back."

"Your mother isn't dead," I said to Vinnie.

"She will be someday," Vinnie said. "Anyway, it got out of hand. In the beginning, I just wanted a short fix to pay Sunflower back on some bad bets, but Sunflower came in and wouldn't let go. Before I knew it, his book-keeper was helping me keep two sets of books."

"Is this the dead book-keeper?"

"Yeah," Vinnie said. "Sudden death with tire tracks on his back."

I thought about Victor Kulik and Walter Dunne, executed behind the diner. Life expectancy with Wellington wasn't good.

Mooner came back with Vinnie's clothes. "I fixed them for you, dude," Mooner said. "They're, like, awesome."

Vinnie stepped into his slacks and looked down at himself. The slacks had been shortened to just below his knees, and his shirt had been turned into a tunic with a rope belt. It went well with his black dress shoes and black socks. Mooner had printed Doderick Bracegirdle with black magic marker on the shirt pocket. Vinnie looked like a wino Hobbit coming off a three-day binge. His gelled hair was stuck every which way, his clothes were wrinkled and smudged with grass stains, his beard belonged to Grizzly Hobbit.

"I'd kill him," Vinnie said, glaring at Mooner, "but you sold my gun."

"Probably, this Drager guy wants to have you arrested for embezzling," I said to Vinnie. "He's not going to care that you're a homeless Hobbit."

"I haven't got a driver's license," Vinnie said. "I haven't got a car."

I hitched my bag onto my shoulder. "I'll take you. Where are we going?"

"He's downtown in the Meagan Building."

The Meagan building was a black glass and steel high-rise built several years before the commercial real estate market crashed. The Wellington Company was on the fifth floor. We stepped out of the elevator into a carpeted hall. Pale gray carpet, cream walls with cherry chair rails and cherrywood doors. Classy. Wellington occupied the entire floor. It was getting to be late in the day and the Wellington front desk was unmanned. Roger Drager was waiting for us in the small reception area.

Drager was in his forties, nicely dressed, had severely receding brown hair, was around 5'10", and his body was going soft. His hand was clammy when we shook.

He led us through a room with cubicles and banks of file cabinets. There were private offices with windows on the perimeter of the room. Doors were open, and most offices were empty. Desks and chairs. Same with the cubicles. Just a few guys slouched back playing computer solitaire. Not much work going on. No phones ringing.

"Where is everyone?" I asked Drager.

"Flex hours," he said. "Most everyone prefers to come in early and leave early."

We followed him down a long hall to his corner office. Large ornate desk and credenza on one side of the office. Seating area with a small couch and two chairs and a coffee table on the other. He directed us to the seating area. So far, he hadn't seemed to notice Vinnie was a Hobbit.

"Let me get right to the point," Drager said to Vinnie. "I know you've been stealing from Wellington. I want full disclosure, and I want the money you've embezzled. I want the names on all the bad bonds you've written."

"Yessir," Vinnie said. "I'll cooperate totally. I don't know where I'll get the money, but I'll pay it back somehow. Are you calling the police in?"

"Not if you repay the money." Drager stood and looked at his watch. "I have another meeting. You can let yourselves out?"

"Absolutely," Vinnie said. "No problem."

Drager walked partially down the hall with us, said goodbye, and entered another office. Vinnie and I continued on toward the room with the cubicles. The building was eerily quiet, with the exception of a room to the right. I could hear machinery working on the other side of the closed door. I opened the door and looked in. There was a large paper shredder working. A bored-looking kid stood beside the shredder. Black garbage bags presumably filled with paper were stacked against a wall.

"What?" the kid said.

"Sorry," I said to him. "Looking for the ladies room."

"By the elevator."

I thanked him and closed the door. I didn't say anything to Vinnie until we got into the car and were out of the parking lot.

"So what do you think?" I asked Vinnie.

"He was nervous," Vinnie said. "Scared."

Vinnie might be a creepy human being, but he was an excellent judge of people. That's one of the reasons Vinnie was a good bail bondsman. Vinnie knew when people were lying, scared, doped-up, dumb, or crazy. When Vinnie wasn't intentionally scamming, he didn't write a lot of bad bonds. Vinnie knew who was going to run and who was going to show up for court.

"Do you have any idea why Drager was nervous?"

"I'm guessing someone's putting pressure on him."

"His next meeting?"

Vinnie shrugged. "All I know is Drager didn't want to shut me down or send me to jail. He just wanted the money."

"You know what else I thought was weird. The office. There weren't any people working there. He said they left early, but I didn't see any clutter on the desks in the empty cubicles and offices. Nothing in their wastebaskets. The only machine working was the paper shredder. What kind of an office has that many empty desks and a giant paper shredder?"

"A fake office," Vinnie said. "Cripes, I don't want to say what I'm thinking."

"That you and Bobby Sunflower have been scamming an even bigger scammer?"

"Yeah."

"Drager?"

"Drager's mixed up in it, but he's not the end of the line. Someone's got his nuts in a vise."

CHAPTER
TWENTY-TWO

Lula and Connie were waiting for us to return to the office, and it was coming up to time for dinner, so I stopped on the way back to get a bucket of chicken. I was getting sick of chicken, but it was easy and fast and relatively cheap.

We took the chicken into Vinnie's inner office, set up more folding chairs, and dug in.

"What did Drager want?" Connie asked.

"Money," Vinnie said. "He wants the money he lost on the phony bonds."

Connie stopped eating. "How much is that?"

"I don't know," Vinnie said. "A lot. Maybe a million. I have to go back over the files."

Connie, Lula, and I exchanged a mental message. The message was *No way, Jose.*

The front door to the office opened and closed, and Connie went to see who'd walked in. I followed after her, and Lula followed after me.

Three men stood in the middle of the office. They were dressed in collared knit shirts left untucked, dark slacks, and scuffed shoes. My first thought was cops. My second was hired goons. They were in their forties, and they all looked like they ate a lot of starch and vodka and didn't get enough sun. Doughy faces, soft bellies. Mean little pig eyes. Receding hairlines. Guns stuck in the waistbands of their slacks, mostly hidden under the knit shirts.

Connie went to her desk and sat down. I knew why. Connie kept the Uzi and a Glock in her middle drawer. Lula and I stood in front of Vinnie's office, and I closed the door behind me.

"Can I help you?" Connie asked.

"We're looking for Vincent Plum."

"He isn't here," Connie said. "Would you like to leave a message?"

"Lady, we saw him walk in here in weird clothes. Tell him Larry, Mo, and Eugene want to talk to him."

"And this would be in reference to what?" Connie asked.

"It's a business matter."

"I'm afraid Mr Plum isn't available right now."

Larry hauled his gun out of his pants. "And I'm afraid I'm going to have to shoot one of you if he doesn't get available."

"Hey, Vinnie," Connie yelled. "There are some idiots here to see you." I stepped aside, and Vinnie stuck his head out.

"What?" Vinnie said.

"You need to come with us," Larry said. "We're going for a ride."

"Are you shitting me?" Vinnie said. "I already took the ride. I'm done with the ride. Sunflower got his money. What's your deal?"

"We pick up and deliver," Larry said. "We don't make the deals. We don't know anything about the deals. And we don't work for Sunflower."

"So who do you work for?" Vinnie asked.

"You find that out when you go for the ride."

"Look at me," Vinnie said. "I'm dressed like a Hobbit. I'm not going for any more rides dressed like a Hobbit."

"What the fuck is a hobbit?" Larry asked.

"They're little people from Middle Earth," I said.

"You mean like midgets?"

"No, but they might be distantly related to Munchkins," I told him.

"What are you on, dopey dust?" Larry said to me.

I didn't actually know what dopey dust was, but I was pretty sure I wasn't on it.

"I'm done talking," Larry said to Vinnie. "I don't care if you're dressed like a turnip. March. The car's out front."

"No," Vinnie said.

And Vinnie jumped back and slammed his door shut and locked it. Mo and Eugene drew their guns, and all three men shot the door full of holes.

"You're in big trouble now," Lula said to the men. "That door's owned by The Wellington Company, and they're gonna be pissed when they see what you did to their door. It's not like doors grow on trees, you know."

"I don't give a rat's ass about The Wellington Company," Larry said.

"Then how about the cops?" Lula said. "Do you worry about them? On account of Vinnie's in there calling the police right now. Or at least he would if he had a phone."

"Kick the door down," Larry said to Eugene.

Connie, Lula, and I knew this wouldn't be an easy thing to do. This wasn't the first time Vinnie had to retreat to his office and hide. Vinnie had the door reinforced with rebar and inch-thick bolts that ran the width of the door.

Eugene gave the door a kick just below the handle. Nothing. He put his shoulder into it. Nothing. He shot the lock and kicked some more. Enough of the wood had splintered off that some of the rebar was showing through.

"He's got this thing reinforced," Eugene said.

"I'm not leaving here empty-handed," Larry said. "We'll take one of the women."

"Whoever the heck you work for won't be happy with that," Lula said. "They want Vinnie. Do any of us look like Vinnie? I don't think so."

"Which one do you want?" Eugene asked. "You want the fat one mouthing off?"

Lula's eyes got so wide they looked like billiard balls. "Excuse me? Did you just say I was fat? Because you better not have said that. I am big and beautiful, but I am not fat. And I don't put up with that slander shit. And I would just like to see you lay one hand on me, because I'll kick your ass from here to Sunday."

"How about if we shoot you," Larry said.

"You'd be in big trouble with The Wellington Company again. They wouldn't have no one to do the filing. Maybe they'd talk to your boss, and he'd make

220

one of you morons come in here to do the filing. Is that what you want? You want to file all day, because it's no picnic."

"You take her and I quit," Eugene said. "She never shuts up."

"I hear you," Larry said. "Take one of the others."

Eugene looked at him. "Which one? How about the one at the desk with the tits."

Now that was insulting. "Hey," I said. "Show some sensitivity. I've got tits, too, you know."

"So take the one with the little tits," Larry said. "I don't care who you take. I just want to get out of here."

"Thanks, but no," I said.

"I thought you were volunteering," Larry said.

"I wasn't volunteering. I was just pointing out that I have tits."

"Grab her," Larry said to Eugene.

I moved fast and put Connie's desk between us. We danced around the desk a couple times, and Larry yelled to stop.

"Here's the way it's going down," Larry said to me. "You go with us, or I'm going to shoot one of your friends."

"What happens if I go with you?"

"I guess we hold you hostage until we can swap you out for the loser in the office."

"That don't sound so bad," Lula said.

"Well, great," I said to Lula. "If you think it sounds so wonderful, you can go with them."

"Nuh-ah," Lula said. "I'm mad at them. Mr Pasty Flabby said I was fat."

Mr Pasty Flabby aimed the gun at Lula and squeezed off a round. The bullet tagged her in the fleshy part of her arm and dug into the wall behind her. Connie opened her desk drawer, grabbed the Glock, and shot Larry in the knee. Larry yelped and went down like a sack of sand.

"Drop your guns, or I'll shoot him again," Connie said.

Eugene and Mo dropped their guns and froze, and Larry rolled around, holding his knee, bleeding through his slacks.

"Get him out of here," Connie said. "And don't come back."

Eugene and Mo dragged Larry out the door, shoved him into their car, and laid rubber driving off.

"That asshole shot me," Lula said. "And now I'm bleeding. Somebody get me a Band-Aid. I'm gonna be real upset if I get blood on this tank top. It was one-of-a-kind at T.J.Maxx. I was lucky to find it."

Bolts slid, and Vinnie's door creaked open. "Are they gone?" Vinnie asked, peeking out.

"Yes," Connie said. "But they'll be back."

"We have a problem," I said. "Where are we going to stash Vinnie?"

"Don't even think about me," Lula said.

"He's your relative," Connie said to me.

"I already took a turn at it," I told her.

"Mooner's out," Connie said. "He's going to be wall-to-wall Hobbits."

I looked at Vinnie. "Well?"

"How about a hotel?" Vinnie said.

222

"No money," Connie told him. "We're totally in the red."

"Don't you have any friends?" I asked Vinnie.

"I only have friends when I have money," Vinnie said.

"That's just sad," Lula said. "You're a pathetic individual."

"Bite me," Vinnie said.

"See, that's what we're talkin' about," Lula said. "You're a hotbed of anger, and since I'm takin' these courses in human nature, I know that comes from insecurity. You probably wet your bed or something. Or maybe you got a little pencil dick, or you can't get it up without sexual enhancement aids. Or maybe you're one of those who got a crook in their penis. It's pretty common, but some men don't like it. Personally, I find a dick that turns a corner can be a unique experience."

"Just shoot me," Vinnie said.

"I'll take him until I find something better," I said, "but both of you owe me. I expect you to come over and clean my bathroom when he leaves."

I deposited Vinnie in my apartment and gave him strict instructions. He was to use his own towels. He was to stay out of my bedroom. My bed was off limits, and my clothes were off limits. He was not to finger my panties. He was not to feed Rex or tap on his cage. He could eat my food and drink my beer as long as he didn't clean me out.

"Sure," Vinnie had said. "Whatever."

I'd changed into a little black skirt, white stretchy top with a low V-neck, black lightweight cardigan sweater, and black heels. Lenny Pickeral, the toilet paper bandit, was going to be at Burt Pickeral's viewing tonight, and I felt compelled to capture Lenny. I'm not sure why, because the bail bonds office wasn't exactly operational. I suppose this was a way to convince myself of some normalcy.

I called to see if Grandma wanted a ride to the viewing.

"That would be wonderful," Grandma said. "Emily Klug was supposed to pick me up, but she's got bleeding hemorrhoids."

Grandma and I got there a half hour after the viewing started, and the lot attached to the funeral home was packed. I dropped Grandma off at the door and watched her stomp and step to the stairs. She had borrowed crutches, and between the crutches and the ortho boot, she was making the most of her broken bone. I parked a block away and did a fast walk back to Stiva's.

The air in the funeral home was heavy with the smell of carnations and lilies. I don't have allergies, but funeral home flowers make my nose run. Too many flowers in too small a space, I suppose, combined with overly perfumed women and Stiva's inadequate ventilation.

The Elks arrived in full regalia with sashes and hats and medallions and hundred-proof breath just as I entered the lobby. I pushed through the crush, looking for Grandma, looking for Lenny Pickeral. Probably, it was a terrible thing to attempt an arrest in the midst of grief, but it was my job, and it was the law. And the truth is, no one in this crowd seemed overwhelmed by the tragedy of Burt's passing. Burt led a long, full life, and the Burg is good at accepting death. Lots of devout Catholics who found genuine solace in their faith.

I heard an exclamation go up in front of me. It was followed by murmuring and some movement. I squeezed my way in and saw Grandma standing over Maria Lorenzo. Two men were trying to get Maria up on her feet, but Maria topped the scales at somewhere around two hundred and fifty pounds, and they were having a hard time figuring out where to grab her.

"Sorry I knocked you down," Grandma said to Maria. "It's these dang crutches. I haven't got the hang of them yet, but I got to use them, because my foot is broke all over. I should be in a wheelchair, but I don't want to look like a sissy."

I eased Grandma away from Maria and moved her into a less congested area. She tagged two people en route, but no one went down.

"Stay here," I said. "You can't do any more damage if you don't move from this spot."

"Yeah, but what good is that? I'm not near the cookies. And I haven't even seen the deceased yet. And people can't see me with my disability over here."

"If you keep hitting people in the back of the leg with your crutches, they'll kick you out."

"They won't do that. I'm an old lady and I'm gonna die soon, and they want my business. I got a real expensive slumber box picked out here. Mahogany with gold handles and padded inside with genuine satin. And it's lead-lined, so the worms won't get to me. They could have buried King Tut in this slumber box, and he'd be good as new."

I hoped the funeral home wasn't counting on collecting Grandma's funeral money any time soon, because I was pretty sure Grandma wasn't ever going to die.

"Maybe you could walk better without the crutches," I said to her.

"I won't get as much sympathy that way. This is my big chance. Other people get heart attacks and kidney stones, and I never get any of that stuff. I'm healthy as a horse. I don't even get the flu. All I got is a broken foot. And it wasn't even broken enough to get us a handicap sticker for the car. I tell you, there's no justice in this world."

"All right, let's compromise. You can hold the crutches, but you can't use them to try to walk."

"I guess that would be okay," Grandma said. "I can't figure them out anyway. I think I swing when I'm supposed to clomp."

"Where do you want to go first?" I asked her.

"I want to see the deceased. And then I want cookies."

CHAPTER
TWENTY-THREE

I got Grandma in the line inching its way to the casket, and I set off to find Lenny Pickeral. After five minutes of circulating through the room, I realized everyone looked like Lenny Pickeral. Even the women. Some Pickerals were older than others, but other than that they were interchangeable.

I stopped a random Pickeral and asked about Lenny.

"I'm looking for Lenny," I said. "Have you seen him?"

"I was just talking to him," she said. "He's here somewhere."

"Did you notice what he was wearing?"

"Dark sports coat and a blue dress shirt."

Great. That described half the Pickerals. I moved to the other side of the room and asked again.

"He's right over there, talking to Aunt Sophie," the woman said. "He has his back to us."

I slipped in next to Lenny and put my hand on his arm. "Lenny Pickeral?" I asked.

He turned and looked at me. "Yeah."

"Excuse us," I said to Aunt Sophie. "I'd like a word with Lenny."

Lenny was my height and slim. His clothes were neat but inexpensive. His skin tone was office worker. I led him to a quiet corner and introduced myself.

"What does that mean?" Lenny asked. "Bond enforcement."

"When you didn't show up for trial, my employer had to forfeit the money he posted for you. If I bring you back to the court to get a new date, we get our money back."

"That sounds okay," Lenny said. "When do you want to do that?"

"Now."

"Will it take long? I drove my mom here."

"Can she get someone else to take her home?"

"I guess. Is there night court? How does this work?"

He was asking too many questions. And I could see the panic pooling in his eyes. He was going to run. I pulled cuffs out of my purse and *click!* One was around his wrist. His eyes got wide, and his mouth dropped open, and he looked at the cuff like it was reptilian.

"I don't want to make a scene. Just quietly and calmly walk out with me," I said.

"What's going on?" a woman said. "Why did you put handcuffs on Lenny? Hey, Maureen, look at this."

In the space of a heartbeat, Lenny and I were surrounded by Pickerals.

"Nothing dramatic going on," I said. "I'm just taking Lenny downtown to reschedule his court date."

"Is this over the toilet paper?" a man asked.

"Yes," I said.

"It's not fair. He gave it all back."

"And it was for a good cause," another man said. "He was protesting. You ever have to use one of them restrooms on the Turnpike? That toilet paper's like wax paper."

Okay, here's the thing. I actually hated the toilet paper in the Turnpike restrooms, so I understood the protest. Problem was, the only thing worse than the wax paper toilet paper was no toilet paper at all.

An older woman bustled in. "I'm his mother. What's this?" she said, taking in the handcuffs.

"It's about the toilet paper," someone said.

"Oh, for goodness sakes," Mrs Pickeral said. "It was toilet paper. And it wasn't even any good."

"Besides, it's his life's work," a woman said. "He's a crusader. He's like Robin Hood."

"Yeah," everyone murmured. "Robin Hood."

"He still has to keep his court date," I told them.

"There's no court tonight," Mrs Pickeral said. "And I need him to give me a ride home. I'll make sure he goes tomorrow morning."

I heard this a lot. No one ever showed up in the morning.

"Look at him," Mrs Pickeral said. "Does he look like a criminal?"

My nose was running and my eyes were feeling puffy from the flowers. And I was caring less and less about Lenny Pickeral and his stupid toilet paper crime spree.

"Fine," I said, unlocking the cuffs. "I'm letting him go, but I'm holding all of you responsible. If Lenny doesn't show up at court tomorrow morning to get rebonded, you'll all be accessories to a crime."

That was a crock of doodie, but I felt like I had to say something. And it was at that instant that God rewarded me for showing compassion and letting Lenny walk. Or maybe it was the bottle that was back in my bag that brought me luck. I turned from Lenny, and from the corner of my eye I caught a glimpse of a head sticking up above the mourning masses. It was Butch Goodey. Lenny's capture fee would have bought me a meatball sub. Goodey's capture fee would pay my rent and then some.

Goodey was up by the casket, paying condolences to the family. I hugged the wall, coming at him from the rear. I had no clue how to take him down. I didn't have a stun gun or pepper spray. I wasn't about to shoot him. Even if I could get the cuffs on him, I didn't think I could stop him from fleeing. I stood to one side and waited for him to move from the casket area.

"Yo," I said, stepping in front of him. "How's it going?"

His expression was blank for a moment while he connected the dots, and then recognition slammed into him.

"You again!" he said, wheeling around, looking for an exit, fixing on the door to the lobby.

"Wait!" I said, grabbing the back of his jacket. "We need to talk. We can deal."

"I'm not going to jail," he said. And he took off for the door. I still had my fingers wrapped into his jacket, and I held tight, trying to slow him down with my weight, not having any luck with it. He was knocking people over, pushing them aside, muscling his way to the lobby.

Grandma was just inside the open double doors, standing beside the cookie station. "Hey!" she said to Butch. "What the heck's going on with you and my granddaughter?"

"Get outta my way," Butch said.

"That's no way to talk to a old lady," Grandma said, and she whacked Butch in the shins with her crutch.

"Ow!" Butch said, stopping just long enough for me to bash him in the gonads with my purse. Butch sucked air, went down to his knees, and doubled over.

I rushed at him with FlexiCuffs and bound his ankles. Twice.

"Boy," Grandma said. "You pack a wallop with that purse. What have you got in it?"

"Uncle Pip's lucky bottle."

Now I had Butch rolling around on the floor of the funeral parlor. I sort of had him captured, but I had no way to get him into my car. I couldn't drag him, and he couldn't walk with his ankles bound. If I cuffed his hands and released the shackles on his ankles, he'd run away.

"I need help getting him to my car," I said to the crowd of people clustered around us.

Everyone shuffled their feet. No one volunteered.

"For goodness sakes," I said. "This man is a felon."

The funeral director, Milton Shreebush, rushed over. "Holy cats," he said, looking down at Butch.

"He's FTA," Grandma said. "My granddaughter just made a bond enforcement maneuver."

"I see that," Milton said. "But he can't stay on the floor like this."

"Then help me drag him to my car," I told him.

Milton reached for Butch, and Butch growled and grabbed him. Milton slapped at Butch, and they rolled around, locked together.

"Help!" Milton yelled. "Get the police. Somebody do something!"

I stepped in and hit Butch in the head with my purse. Butch shook his head, stunned, and Milton scrambled away.

"That didn't work so good," Grandma said.

Butch was crabbing around, waving his arms, trying to grab people, and everyone was keeping their distance. I figured my choices were hit him with the bottle and knock him out, call the police, call RangeMan, or let him go. I decided to go with RangeMan.

It took RangeMan five minutes to respond to my call for help. Two big guys wearing RangeMan black uniforms and full utility belts calmly walked up to Butch and looked at him. Butch was still on the floor, sweating and snarling and spitting and making threatening grabbing motions.

One of the men gave Butch a bunch of volts with a stun gun. The RangeMan guy didn't move fast enough, and Butch grabbed the gun and threw it across the room.

"Hunh," the RangeMan guy said.

"Yeah," I said. "Been there, done that."

"Are you sure he's human?"

"Maybe you could hook a chain to the FlexiCuffs on his ankles and drag him behind your car," I said.

"We tried that once, and Ranger didn't like it," the guy said. "You do something twice that Ranger doesn't like, and you're out of a job and damaged."

"We need to clear the area," the other guy said. "Get rid of the audience."

Most of the gawkers had gotten bored and moved on, and I was able to persuade the few remaining to think about refreshments. I was guiding them to the cookie table, and I heard a sound like a baseball bat hitting a sack of sand. *Thwack!* I turned and saw that Butch was sleeping.

"Is he okay?" I asked them.

"Yeah," the RangeMan guy said. "He'll be fine. He just had to calm down. Would you like us to deliver him to the police station for you?"

"Yes. That would be great," I said.

They cuffed Butch's massive hands behind his back and dragged him away.

"They seem like nice young men," Grandma said.

I took Grandma home and called Ranger.

"Have you got a minute?" I asked him.

"As many as you need."

I drove to the center of the city, turned onto Ranger's street, and parked in the RangeMan garage. I took the elevator to the seventh floor and pressed the intercom button next to Ranger's door. I could have just gone in. I had a key, but I thought that might send the wrong message.

Ranger opened his door and looked me over. "Pretty."

"Thank you. I was at a viewing."

"I heard."

He was still dressed from work. Black T-shirt, black cargo pants, black running shoes. Five o'clock shadow. His apartment was always cool and pristine. Subdued lighting in the hall. Fresh flowers on the narrow hall table. All the work of his housekeeper. I followed him to the kitchen, and he poured me a glass of red wine. His kitchen was small but state-of-the-art. Stainless steel and black granite.

"What are the minutes about?" he asked. "Is this visit personal or business?"

"Business." I sipped the wine. "Nice," I said.

Morelli would have offered me a beer. Ranger always offered me wine I couldn't afford to buy. Ranger knew the value of temptation and bribery.

Ranger leaned against the kitchen counter, arms crossed over his chest. "I'm guessing this is about Vinnie."

"We managed to raise the money to buy back his debt, and we were all at the office and the president of Wellington called and said he wanted to talk to Vinnie."

"This was today?"

"Yes. This afternoon. So Vinnie and I went to Wellington. The offices are in the Meagan Building. And the offices were empty. The president, Roger Drager, was there, and a couple guys in suits playing online solitaire, and a kid working a giant paper shredder. Drager said the company was on flex hours, but the cubicles and offices didn't look used to me. No clutter, nothing in wastebaskets. And Drager was nervous. His hands were sweaty."

"What did he want?"

"Money. He knew about the phony bonds, and he wanted his money back."

"He didn't shut Vinnie down? Didn't go to the police?"

"No. Vinnie said the setup looked fishy. Like it was a shell company. He was worried he was scamming someone who was an even bigger scammer."

"That's not good," Ranger said.

"It gets worse. We got back to the office and three goons came in and tried to snatch Vinnie at gunpoint. One of them shot Lula, but it just knicked her, and then Connie shot one of them in the knee and they left."

Ranger smiled. "Connie's probably been shooting men in the knee since she was twelve."

"So what do you think about Wellington?"

"I think I wouldn't want to work for them."

"Should I go to Morelli?"

"Only if you want second best," Ranger said.

"I'm talking about police action."

Ranger took my wine from me, tasted it, and set it on the counter. "Let's look in on Wellington."

"Now?"

"Yes."

I followed him through his living room into his bedroom.

"The building will be empty," Ranger said, moving into his dressing room. "The cleaning crew should be gone by now."

"What about the alarm?"

"RangeMan installed the security system in the Meagan Building."

CHAPTER
TWENTY-FOUR

Ranger's bedroom was masculine luxury. Dark woods, ivory walls, tans and browns, king-size bed with expensive Italian linens. There was a large bath en suite and a walk-in dressing room as big as my bedroom. He opened a drawer in the built-in dresser, removed a utility belt, and buckled it on. He selected a gun from another drawer. Handcuffs, stun gun, defense spray. He handed me a penlight and took one for himself. He shrugged into a windbreaker with the RangeMan logo clearly visible. He selected a second RangeMan jacket and handed it to me. "Swap your sweater out for this. If someone sees us, I can say we're doing a security check."

We rode the elevator to the garage, where Ranger chose a fleet SUV. The Meagan Building was only blocks away. Easy to find on-street parking at this time of the night. We parked directly in front of the door. Ranger used his fob to enter the building and to diffuse the alarm. No need for the penlight. The lobby was dimly lit, as were the halls and elevator.

"Fifth floor," I told Ranger.

We entered the elevator, he pushed the button, and he looked over at me. "You're very calm," he said.

"It's easy to be calm when I'm with you. I feel protected."

"I try," Ranger said. "You don't always cooperate."

The doors opened, and we walked the hall to Wellington's door. Ranger fobbed it open, we stepped inside and closed the door behind us. The interior room was pitch-black. No path lighting. The outside offices showed ambient light but not enough to guide me. Ranger clicked his penlight on.

"Let's try to use just the one light," he said. "Hang on to me if you can't see."

I curled my hand into the back of his cargo pants just above his gun belt. "I'm good to go."

He was still for a beat. "You could have held on to my jacket," he said.

"Would you rather I do that?"

"No. Not even a little."

He flicked the light over the cubicles and into the offices. He stopped and opened a file cabinet. Empty.

"You were right," he said. "None of this is being used. Where's Drager's office?"

"There's a hall at the end of this room. His office is at the end of the hall."

Ranger flicked the light at the shredder room door. "What's in here?"

"Paper shredder."

"And this one?"

"It's an office. Drager said he had a meeting. He went into this office, and we let ourselves out."

Ranger opened the door and flashed the light around. It was a boardroom. Large oval table. Chairs pulled up to the table. Unoccupied at the moment.

We continued down the hall to Drager's office. The door was ajar, and Ranger stopped before entering. He knew what he was going to find inside. I did, too. We could smell it. Decomposing body. It doesn't take long after death. The body evacuates. Blood pools. The smell is unmistakable.

"Wait here," Ranger said.

"It's okay," I told him. "I can deal."

Drager was on the floor by his desk. Probably fell out of his chair. Bullet to the back of his head. Execution-style. Like Kulik and Dunne. Ranger pulled on disposable gloves and methodically went through the file cabinets.

"I'm not finding anything here," he said. "This office has been stripped." He moved to the credenza. "Uh-oh," he said when he opened the top drawer.

"What uh-oh? I hate uh-oh."

"Leave the room."

"Excuse me?"

"Explosives," Ranger said. "On a timer and a trip wire. If I'd opened the drawer another half inch, your hamster would be an orphan."

"How much time do we have?"

"Seven minutes."

"Shit!"

I turned and tripped over Drager's briefcase.

"Take it," Ranger said, grabbing my hand, yanking me forward into the hall.

We ran flat out down the hall and through the room with the cubicles. We burst out the door and ran to the elevator. Ranger had it on hold. It was still at our floor.

We jumped into the elevator, and Ranger hit the button for the ground floor.

"How much time do we have?" I asked him.

"Four minutes," he said. "Plenty of time."

We exited the elevator into the lobby, crossed the lobby, and left the building. Ranger reset the alarm with the fob, and we got into the SUV.

"Two minutes," Ranger said, pulling away from the curb.

The fifth-floor windows blew out when we reached the corner. Ranger hooked a U-turn and parked so we could watch the building. There was a second explosion, the alarm was wailing away, and fire spilled out the open windows.

Ranger called his control room. "Tell all responders to the Meagan Building alarm to secure the exterior of the building. Under no circumstances are they to go inside until the fire marshall declares the building safe."

Two RangeMan SUVs arrived and parked half a block from the burning building. A police car was simultaneously on the scene. Ranger made another U-turn and drove back to RangeMan. He parked in the garage and looked over at me.

"You can really haul ass in those heels," he said. "The memory will give me sleepless nights for a long time."

That got a smile out of me. "Sorry to interfere with your sleep."

"There's a solution to the problem," Ranger said, getting out of the car. "You can finish your wine upstairs, and we can discuss it." He opened the passenger-side door, took the briefcase from me, and grinned. "Babe, you have panic written all over your face."

"You're a dilemma."

He ushered me into the elevator. "Good to know."

We rode in silence to Ranger's floor, he opened his door, and I went to the kitchen and retrieved my wine.

"I would have liked more time at Wellington," Ranger said.

He dropped his jacket and gun belt onto the kitchen counter, poured a glass of wine for himself, and refreshed mine.

"They were shredding bags of papers when I was there with Vinnie. Probably, there wasn't anything left to see."

Ranger took his wine into the dining room and dumped the contents of Drager's briefcase onto the table.

"Bank statements," Ranger said. "And a list of businesses owned by the firm." He leafed through the bank statements. "Looks like a pattern of outgoing wire transfers to a New Jersey LLC called GBZakhar, and someone has checked them off on the latest statement."

He took the statement to the combination office and den attached to his bedroom and typed Zakhar into his computer.

"GBZakhar doesn't have a web site," he said. "Let's go to the Jersey state business gateway site."

Ranger worked his way through the site and finally came to a guide for requesting public record information. He gave a credit card number, and information on GBZakhar was displayed on the screen.

"This is interesting," Ranger said. "Do you recognize the name of the registered agent?"

"Walter Dunne. One of the Wellington lawyers found executed behind the diner."

"GBZakhar gives a Newark PO box as its address. And they list four company officers. Herpes Zoster, Mickey Mouskovitch, Rainbow Trout, and Gregor Bluttovich. I expect the first three names are fake. That leaves Gregor Bluttovich," Ranger said.

"Blutto! Gritch said he heard Sunflower talk about Blutto. Gritch didn't know if it was a first name, last name, or nickname."

I was leaning over the back of Ranger's chair, reading off the computer screen, trying hard not to kiss his neck. It would be absolutely the wrong thing to do, but it was so tempting. He always smelled great, like his Bulgari Green shower gel. How it stayed with him all day was a mystery. His black T-shirt spanned his biceps. He wore a watch as his only jewelry. His back looked athletic under his shirt. I thought it would look even better without the shirt. All I had to do was touch my lips to his neck, and the shirt would be gone.

"Babe," Ranger said, "if you don't back up a couple inches, we're going to be finding out about Bluttovich in the morning."

I didn't move. I was contemplating.

"Babe?"

I stepped away from his chair. "I was reading the screen. Let's see what you can pull up on Blutto."

Ranger had state-of-the-art computer programs that left most people with virtually no secrets. He could get medical records, credit histories, shoe size, litigation, you name it.

Ranger plugged Gregor Bluttovich into one of the programs and information scrolled up.

"Fifty-two years old," Ranger said. "Born in Varna, Bulgaria. Came to this country in '92. He has four ex-wives and is currently unmarried. He has seven kids distributed among his ex-wives. The oldest is thirty-four. The youngest is six. He was a police officer in Varna for fifteen years. No work history after that. He owns property in Newark and Bucks County. I know the Newark area. It has a large Russian immigrant population. The Bucks County property is in Taylorsville. He's affiliated with three other holding companies. He had a double bypass two years ago. He was charged with assault with a deadly weapon last year, but the charges were dropped."

"What was the weapon?"

"A chain saw. He cut a guy's leg off. He claimed it was an accident."

"This is not a nice man."

"I have a couple contacts in Newark. See if you can find some crackers and cheese in the kitchen, and I'll make some phone calls."

I went to the kitchen and poured myself another glass of wine. I found some brie and something else that was creamy and herby. I'm sure all bought by his housekeeper, Ella. I put the two cheese wedges on a cutting board with water crackers, apple slices, and fresh strawberries and brought them in to Ranger, along with the bottle of wine and our glasses. I set everything on Ranger's desk, and I spread brie on a cracker for myself.

Ranger took his headset off. "This is nice."

"I take no responsibility. Ella had everything prepared."

Ranger sliced off some mystery cheese and ate it with an apple slice. No empty-calories cracker for Ranger. Ranger was into health.

"I talked to two people in Newark," Ranger said. "The opinion of both is that Gregor Bluttovich is dangerous. Bulgarian mobster. Nicknamed Blutto. Large ego. Terrible temper. Probably criminally insane. Both contacts used the word *psycho* to describe Bluttovich. He has a mid-size operation, and he's overextended. Word on the street is that he's eliminating squeamish business partners."

"Like Wellington?"

"Yes."

"Where would Vinnie fit in this?"

"Bluttovich owns Wellington. So Vinnie scammed Bluttovich. And it's not healthy to scam Bluttovich."

"How not healthy?"

"As not healthy as you can get."

"Dead?"

"Very dead," Ranger said.

"What am I supposed to do?"

"Have another glass of wine."

"And then?"

Ranger's eyes locked onto mine.

244

"If I didn't know better, I'd think you were trying to get me drunk," I said to Ranger.

"Not drunk," Ranger said. "Just relaxed and naked."

I was distracted by an icon blinking on his computer screen.

"Why is the little flame flashing?" I asked him.

"I'm hard-wired to the control room. One of our systems just sent in a fire alert."

He tapped a key and an address appeared.

"Hamilton Avenue," I said. "Omigod, that's the bonds office!"

Ranger put his headset on and talked to the control room, verifying the fire. He took his headset off, swiveled away from his desk, and stood.

"I suppose this is the end of our romantic moment," I said to him.

"It's okay," he said. "You'll have a lot more opportunities for romantic moments."

He closed the space between us and kissed me. Our tongues touched, and I pressed against him.

"It's only a fire," I whispered.

He paused for a beat. "You've seen one, you've seen them all," he said. And he stripped my white stretchy shirt off. He kissed me again, and when he broke from the kiss, my eyes inadvertently strayed to the computer screen. "Babe?"

"I can't help it. All those blinking things on your computer are distracting."

He reached over, hit a key, and the screen went black.

"I know they're there," I said.

Ranger tugged my shirt back over my head and smoothed it down. "I'm good and I'm motivated, but I know enough not to try to please a woman who's distracted." He kissed me lightly on the lips and pointed me toward the kitchen. "You owe me."

I grabbed my purse and black cardigan, and Ranger buckled his gun belt back on. We rode the elevator to the garage and took my Mercedes SUV, with Ranger driving.

"This car smells like fried chicken," Ranger said. "And something else that isn't good."

"Connie's stink bomb," I told him.

CHAPTER
TWENTY-FIVE

Ranger turned onto Hamilton, and I could see the glow from the fire. My breath caught in my chest and my eyes filled with tears.

"Call Connie and Lula and Vinnie and make sure they're okay," Ranger said.

I dialed Connie first. She answered on the second ring, and I breathed a little easier. I told her about the fire, and told her to stay home until I got back in touch. I called Lula next. She was home as well. I called my apartment twice before Vinnie picked up.

"I didn't know if I was supposed to answer your phone," Vinnie said.

"I wanted to make sure you were okay. The bonds office is on fire."

"Crap!" Vinnie said. "I'll be right there."

"No! I just got here with Ranger. We'll handle it. I don't want you to leave the apartment."

"How bad is it?"

"It's bad. I'll call you back when I know more."

Ranger parked a block away, and it was difficult to see much of anything other than billowing smoke and flames shooting into the black sky. The street was clogged with fire trucks, EMTs, and police cars. Men shouted instructions. They were already getting water to the fire, but the closer we got, the more it became apparent that nothing was going to be saved. There was a series of small explosions and everyone pulled back.

"Ammo," Ranger said.

Thank goodness we had the yard sale, I thought. The ammo that was left was minimal. And the dynamite had all gotten cleared out. The explosions stopped and the firefighters moved closer. They were concentrating on containment and minimizing the damage to adjoining properties.

"This is out of control," Ranger said. "We're going to have to do something about Bluttovich."

"Like what?"

"Short-term, we need to encourage him to forget Vinnie. Long-term, we need to neutralize him. Provide law enforcement with a reason to put Bluttovich away for a very long time."

Ranger's attention shifted off me. I turned to see what caught his eye and spotted Morelli walking toward us.

"There's no need for you to stay to the end here," Ranger said. "Let Morelli follow you home, just in case Blutto's watching. I'll stay to talk to the fire marshall."

"You don't have to stay," I said.

"It's my job," Ranger said. "RangeMan manages security on the bonds office."

Morelli ambled over. He nodded to Ranger as Ranger walked off to find the fire marshall, and he gave me a tight smile. "Are you okay?" he asked me.

"Yes," I said. "The fire trucks were already here when I arrived."

"That's a relief," Morelli said. "I was half afraid you and Lula started the fire." He looked around. "It wasn't Lula, was it?"

"No," I said. "I checked."

Morelli looked me over. "That's your viewing uniform."

"Yes, and the heels are killing me. I'm ready to go home. Would you mind following me? Ranger thinks I need an escort."

I detoured around the fire, and twenty minutes later, I rolled into my apartment parking lot with Morelli on my bumper. We got out of our cars, and Morelli walked me into the building.

I took my shoes off and pushed the elevator button.

"Probably, I should walk you all the way to your door," Morelli said. "Maybe I should even go inside and check under your bed for monsters."

The elevator doors opened, and Vinnie was standing there wearing my panties.

"Going up?" he asked.

Morelli's jaw dropped. "What the hell?"

"I got locked out," Vinnie said. "I went downstairs to do my laundry, and when I got back to the apartment, the door was closed shut."

"Those are my panties," I said.

Vinnie looked down at himself. "I figured you wouldn't want me running around naked. All my clothes are in the washer."

"And you decided panties were the way to go?" I asked.

"It was the only thing that fit. They got elastic."

"Lucille kicked him out, and he didn't have any place to stay," I told Morelli.

Morelli grinned at me. "I've seen you in those panties, and they look a lot better when you wear them."

"How's the bonds office?" Vinnie wanted to know.

"Burned to the ground," I said.

"Oh jeez!" Vinnie said. "Crap. Shit. Damn." He punched the elevator wall and stamped his foot.

"This isn't a good picture," Morelli said.

"Yeah, and I don't want the underwear back, either," I said.

"Maybe you should come home with me, and let Vinnie have the apartment to himself," Morelli said.

I bit into my lower lip. I left Vinnie alone in my apartment for a few hours, and he was wearing my panties when I came home. I got stomach cramps thinking about what might happen if I left him overnight.

"That's probably not a good idea," I said to Morelli. "I can't afford to throw away any more underwear."

"Understood. I hate to leave you on a sinking ship, but I don't know what more I can do here, unless you want me to arrest him for indecent exposure," Morelli said. He grabbed me and kissed me, moved me back two steps into the elevator, and pushed the button for the second floor. "Let me know when he leaves. We can go shopping and replace the underwear with something really skimpy."

Vinnie and I got off at the second floor, and I let us into my apartment.

"You can't walk around like that," I said to Vinnie. "You're freaking me out." I rummaged through my closet and came up with an old robe.

"I saw that," Vinnie said, "but I didn't think I'd look good in it."

"Have you seen yourself in the panties? It's why people go blind. Not only don't they fit, but you're all lumpy. It's a hideous sight."

"Cripes," Vinnie said. "Just tell me how you feel."

I held the robe out to him.

Vinnie put the robe on and got a beer out of the fridge. "I bet that fire was arson."

"Without a doubt."

"Drager is going to be pissed. Has anybody called him? Do you think I should call?"

I went dead still for a moment, thinking about Drager's lifeless body lying on his office floor. And then the explosion that had to have obliterated not only all evidence of The Wellington Company, but also of Drager.

"I imagine RangeMan will get in touch with Wellington," I said. "I don't think it's necessary for you to call."

"I feel like an orphan," Vinnie said. "I haven't got Lucille, and I haven't got my office. I haven't even got my own underwear."

251

I know he made all his own problems, but I felt sorry for him anyway. "Get another beer and we'll see if we can find a movie to watch."

By the time I went to bed, Vinnie had retrieved his clothes from the dryer downstairs and was out of my bathrobe. I put the robe in my hamper and told him he could keep the panties. I think he was pleased.

At nine in the morning, Lula, Connie, Vinnie, and I all showed up at the office as if it existed. The fire trucks, EMTs, and police cars were gone, but sooty water still pooled in the gutter. Three buildings were cordoned off with crime-scene tape. The bookstore on one side of the bonds office and the dry cleaner on the other side showed no structural damage. They were smoke-smudged and water-logged, but they were standing intact. The bonds office was a pile of charred rubble.

"Ain't this a bitch," Lula said. "My couch is gone. Where am I gonna sit?"

"The office can get rebuilt," Connie said, "but we've lost years of files that we'll never be able to replace. Phone numbers, addresses, open bonds. They're all gone."

"Good riddance," Vinnie said. "I was in debt up to my gonads. We can make a fresh start."

"Yeah," Lula said. "We can buy a new couch. We could get one that vibrates."

"Reality check," I said. "Burning down the office wasn't a friendly gesture. Remember the three men who wanted to kidnap Vinnie but were willing to settle for me? They're still out there. They probably burned down the office."

"Only two of them," Lula said. "Larry got a bum knee."

"My favorite nail polish was in my desk drawer," Connie said. "I'm going to have to buy new nail polish."

"This here's real sad," Lula said. "I don't know where I'm supposed to go. Do I have a job?"

"I'll call The Wellington Company," Connie said. "It's Saturday, but there might be someone working. I'm sure they'll just move the bonds business into a different location."

We all waited while Connie tapped the number in and listened for the connection.

"It's not a working number," Connie said a minute later.

"What's with that?" Lula wanted to know.

"It's the only number I have for them," Connie said. "I don't have any cell numbers. Maybe we should go downtown and see if anyone's working. If I was Drager, and one of my buildings burned down, I'd be at my desk this morning."

"I'll drive," I said.

I knew Drager wasn't going to be at his desk, but I didn't want to share that information and have to explain my break-in with Ranger. If I drove everyone downtown, they'd see for themselves. Not to mention I had no idea what else to do. I felt like I was floating in space with no direction. Everyone packed into my SUV, and I took Hamilton to Broad.

"You know what we should do?" Lula said. "We should open our own bail bonds agency. We could call it Big and Beautiful Bail Bonds."

"You need start-up money to do that," Vinnie said. "You need money to rent an office. Security deposits. Advance money for the lease. We'd have to buy computers and software, file cabinets, staplers."

"We could get a loan," Lula said. "Who's got credit?"

"Not me," I said. "I'm a month behind on my rent. I can't get a loan to buy a new car."

"Not me," Vinnie said. "I don't even have credit with my bookie."

"Hell," Lula said. "That's the understatement of the year. Your bookie wants to kill you."

"I could go to my family," Connie said.

We all declined on that one. If we took money from Connie's family, we'd be owned by the Mob.

"What about you?" Vinnie asked Lula.

"I'm in collection," Lula said. "I overextended a little. I'm worried someone's gonna come repossess my shoes."

The Meagan Building was a block away, and my stomach was in a knot. I stopped for a light, and it was obvious traffic was slow ahead. Only one lane was open. The other was barricaded. The light changed, and I crept up to the Meagan Building. Yellow crime-scene tape blocked off the sidewalk. A fire truck and the fire marshall's SUV was parked nearby. There was a lot of charred debris on the sidewalk in front of the building, and four guys in hard hats stood talking. They were standing in the road, looking up at the Meagan

254

Building. The windows on the fifth floor were completely blown out. Black soot covered the exterior of the top floors, and the lower floors were grime-streaked.

"What floor was The Wellington Company on?" Lula asked.

"The fifth floor," I told her.

"Guess we know why they aren't answering their phone," Lula said.

Connie looked out her window. "Someone was really busy last night."

"This is crazy," Vinnie said. "Even the Mob knows enough not to blow up two businesses in one night. Who the heck's doing this?"

"I don't know," Lula said, "but I need chicken. I need doughnuts. I need one of them extra-greasy breakfast muffins with ham and eggs and shit."

CHAPTER
TWENTY-SIX

I stopped at three different drive-thru windows, and by the time we got back to the office, we were all feeling sick, not just from the freakish turn our lives had taken, but also from the food we'd managed to snarf down en route.

"I don't feel so good," Lula said. "I think I must have got a bad egg. I need a Rolaid."

"You know what I need?" Vinnie said. "Lucille. I know this is stupid, but I miss Lucille. I never thought I'd say that. She was such a pain in the ass. How can you miss someone that's a pain in the ass?"

"My ex-husband was a pain in the ass," Connie said, "and I don't miss him at all."

"Ditto for me," I said.

My marriage lasted about fifteen minutes. I caught my ex-husband naked on my dining-room table with Joyce Barnhardt riding him like she was in the Kentucky Derby going for the win.

"Your problem is you're a jerk," Lula said to Vinnie. "You got all normal feelings. Like, you love Lucille. But you can't help from being a jerk. I mean, what kind of a man has a romantic relationship with a duck?"

"I don't know," Vinnie said. "Seemed like a good idea at the time."

"You see?" Lula said. "It's always a good idea at the time. But you don't connect the dots between the good idea and the bad ever after. You got no sense of consequences. I learned all about this in my deviant behavior class at the community college."

"I didn't know you were going to college," Vinnie said.

"Of course you didn't, on account of you don't listen. You're not a listener like me. You'd be a better person if you were a listener."

"I'd listen more if you talked less," Vinnie said.

"Hunh," Lula said. "Your ass."

The crime-scene tape had been stretched across wooden barricades placed close to what used to be the building housing the bonds office. The sidewalk was still passable, and there was still on-street parking. Lula's Firebird was at the curb, along with Connie's car and the Love Bus. Mooner and the Hobbits were on the sidewalk, looking at the rubble.

I parked in front of the Firebird, and walked back to Mooner.

"Dude," Mooner said. "Someone was smoking in bed."

"Yeah," I said. "Not much left of the bonds office."

"Too bad," Mooner said. "I was gonna plug in. The Hobbits need computer juice."

"I have to do my blog," one of the Hobbits said. "I have to Twitter."

257

"Bungo Goodchild," an old Hobbit said. "Where are your manners? Introduce us to this lovely creature."

Mooner pointed to the old Hobbit. "This is Oldbuck of Buckland. He's, like, the oldest dude, but he's cool. The little guy standing next to him is Poppy Proudfoot. Then there's Fredoc Broadbeam. That's, like, self-explanatory. Twofoot of Nobottle. Fauxfrodo. And Chicaribbit."

"That's a lot of Hobbits," Lula said.

"Tell me about it," Mooner said. "It's like I need rubber walls on the old bus. And I can't bake brownies fast enough for these dudes. They sure love their brownies."

The Hobbits were all dressed in a mix of shabby chic Hobbit clothes and assorted footgear. Brown hooded capes, green or brown vests over tunics. Peddle pusher-type pants cinched in with a variety of belts from rope to lizard. Chicaribbit was a girl Hobbit, and her purse matched her pink Converse sneakers. Fredoc Broadbeam was as wide as he was tall. Twofoot of Nobottle was a tall, gangly guy with sandy blond hair and a scraggly beard. Fauxfrodo was nineteen or twenty and covered with tattoos and piercings. And Poppy Proudfoot was the youngest. I was guessing he was seventeen or eighteen.

"How long are the Hobbits going to be with you?" I asked Mooner.

"A week. Hobbit Con starts today, but it doesn't really start to swing until Tuesday when The High Holy One proclaims it officially in session."

"I need to charge my phone," Poppy said. "My mom's going to freak if she can't call me."

"Me, too," Oldbuck said. "My wife will think I'm fooling around if I don't answer my phone."

"You can plug in at my place," I said.

What the heck, I didn't have anything else to do.

"Did you hear that?" Mooner said to the Hobbits. "We have juice! Ysellyra Thorney is going to let all you dudes plug in."

"Three cheers for Ysellyra," Broadbeam said.

"Hobbit hooray!" they all yelled. "Hooray! Hooray!"

"Let's do it again," Poppy said.

"Not necessary," I told them. "Get in the bus and follow me."

"Boy, Hobbits know how to have a good time," Lula said. "Don't take much to make them happy."

I drove across town with the Love Bus on my tail. I parked in the lot to my building, and we all trooped into the elevator. Twofoot, Poppy, Broadbeam, Oldbuck, Fauxfrodo, Chicaribbit, Mooner, Vinnie, and me.

"There are a lot of Hobbits in this elevator," Vinnie said. "Anybody know the weight limit?"

Mooner pushed the button for the second floor and the elevator creaked and shuddered and slowly rose.

"We have lift-off," Mooner said.

"Hobbit Hooray!" they all yelled. "Hooray! Hooray!"

"This could get old," Vinnie said to me. "They're just plugging in, right? Like, an hour and they're gone?"

I unlocked my door and the Hobbits rushed in. They plugged their phones and their laptops into outlets all over the apartment. They used the bathroom, tested out the couch, turned the television on, cooed over Rex, looked in my refrigerator and cupboards.

I found a relatively quiet corner and called Ranger.

"What's all that noise?" Ranger asked. "It sounds like you're having a party."

"It's Hobbits," I said. "They're using my electric. I saw the Meagan Building this morning. There was a lot of damage. Will they have to raze the building?"

"I don't know. They're checking the structural integrity. The bonds office burned like it was made out of cardboard. Ten minutes after you left, the roof went down. Whoever set the fire must have used a decent amount of accelerant."

"Do you think this is the end of it?"

"If Bluttovich destroyed both businesses to cover his tracks, it'll end here. That would be the good business decision. If this has become a personal vendetta against Vinnie, it's probably not over."

"Hard to believe Vinnie is that important to Bluttovich. He doesn't even know Vinnie."

"From what I can tell, Bluttovich is a power-hungry maniac. If he thinks Vinnie is a threat, he'll take him down."

"Where do we go from here?"

"I have men working on it. I'll get back to you in a couple hours."

I disconnected and went to the kitchen for a soda. Mooner was watching Rex. Everyone else was in front of the television, except Vinnie.

"Where's Vinnie?" I asked Mooner.

"Bathroom."

The doorbell rang, and Mooner answered.

I looked out from the kitchen and saw two guys.

"Vincent Plum?" the one guy asked.

"No, dude," Mooner said. "I'm, like, the Moon Man. I'm Bungo."

"Cripes," the guy said. "He's stoned."

"He's the right height. Brown hair. Slim weasel body," the other guy said. "Hit him."

I saw the guy's arm extend with the stun gun, and I ran for Mooner. I reached the door just as Mooner collapsed, and I got tagged, too.

By the time my brain unscrambled, I was tied hands and feet and had duct tape across my mouth. I was rolling around on the floor of a van, bumping into Mooner, who was also bound and taped. It was a panel van with solid sides and two doors in the rear with small windows. The driver and his partner were up front. I didn't want to go there. I could mostly see sky through the windows. A streetlight flashed by. A tree. No way of knowing where we were going. The driver and his partner weren't talking.

The van turned from a smooth road to a bumpy road, hooked a corner, and the road was smooth again. It came to a stop, and the rear doors opened. Mo and Eugene looked in at Mooner and me.

"What the hell's this?" Mo asked.

The driver came around. "What do you mean? It's Vincent Plum and some girl. She got in the way, so we took her, too. She looks like fun."

261

"That's not Vincent Plum, you moron."

"How do you know? Have you ever seen Vincent Plum?"

"I saw him when he stuck his head out of his office. We followed him and the girl from the bonds office to the apartment. That's how we knew where to find them. We would have snatched him then, but Larry was whining and bleeding all over the place."

Eugene joined the group and looked in at Mooner and me. "What the fuck's this?"

"Exactly," Mo said.

"We took the wrong guy," the driver said.

"No shit," Eugene said.

"How was I to know? He's the right height. He's got brown hair. He's sort of weasely."

"Gregor is going to be pissed," Eugene said. "We already called and told him we had Vinnie. He's coming out to personally cut off his nuts."

"Call him and tell him we made a mistake," the driver said.

"What are you, crazy?" Eugene said. "Remember what happened to Ziggy when he brought Gregor the wrong Dairy Queen Blizzard?"

"Yeah," the driver said. "Gregor hit him in the head with a hammer, and now Ziggy falls over when he takes a leak."

"I got an idea," Eugene said. "Why don't we douse the van with gasoline, set it on fire, and shove it off a cliff? Then we tell Gregor there was a faulty gas pedal, and the van went out of control and crashed, and we all

262

got out just in time, except we couldn't rescue Vincent."

"That might work," Mo said.

"Wait a minute," the driver said. "We don't have to get all that elaborate. Has Gregor ever seen Vincent Plum?"

"Not that I know," Eugene said.

"Then what's the problem?" the driver said. "We tell him this is Vincent Plum. That way, Gregor gets to cut someone's nuts off, and he won't be disappointed that he made the trip out here."

"Yeah, but this guy will tell Gregor he's not Plum," Mo said.

The driver shrugged. "We'll leave the tape on his mouth."

"Gregor won't like that," Eugene said. "He likes when people scream and beg."

"So we wait until Gregor starts working on him," the driver said, "and then we take the tape off when this guy's in the screaming stage."

Everyone thought about that for a beat.

"It could work," Mo said.

Eugene agreed.

"Okay, so we have a plan," Eugene said. "Let's haul these two into the house. We'll put them in the tower room. When Gregor gets here, we'll take this guy to the kitchen, because it has a tile floor for easy clean-up. And then we'll save the girl for ourselves for later."

"Mmmrmph," Mooner said.

"Don't worry about it," Eugene said to Mooner. "It only hurts in the beginning, and then you faint."

I was dragged out of the van, and Mo put me over his shoulder like a bag of sand. This was the first chance I had to see the house and its surroundings. There was a large lawn surrounding the house. Beyond the lawn, there were dense trees. Long, paved driveway leading to the house. The house itself could hardly be called a house. It was a fortress. It was ominous gray stone and huge. It defied description. It had a tower with turrets, like a medieval castle. If I had to imagine a house for a Bulgarian maniacal mobster, this would be it.

CHAPTER
TWENTY-SEVEN

We were carried inside and up to the tower room. The bindings were cut away from our ankles but left on our wrists. The tape was ripped off our mouths.

"Gregor won't be here for a while," Eugene said, "so make yourself comfortable." And he closed and locked the door.

"I like my nuts," Mooner said. "I don't want them cut off. I'd be, like, nutless then."

"Don't worry," I said. "We'll get rescued."

"Do you think?"

"Sure." Truth is, I didn't have a lot of faith in a rescue. Time was too short. Ranger was good, but this would require a miracle. I looked around the tower room. Not a lot going on. Stone floor. Circular stone walls ringed by long, narrow windows without panes. Thick wood door that didn't give when I kicked it.

I went to a window and looked out. The house was on a hill surrounded by woods. I could see the Delaware River in the distance. I was pretty sure I was in Pennsylvania. I paced the room for an hour, burning off nervous energy. Mooner was quiet, sitting on the floor, chanting softly.

"Ohmm mooon," he said, eyes closed. "Ohmm mooon."

Another hour went by, and I saw a car turn into the driveway. It was a big black Lincoln Town Car. It rolled to a stop in front of the house, and the driver got out. Large man, dark wiry hair streaked with gray. Couldn't see much of his face from where I stood in the tower. I suspected it was Gregor Bluttovich. Mooner was still convening with his inner self. I didn't want to disturb him. I think he'd made peace with the fact he was going to lose his nuts, and I don't think it occurred to him that death would follow.

After a couple minutes, there were loud voices on the stairs, accompanied by heavy footsteps. The tower door banged open, jolting Mooner out of his contemplative state, filling me with renewed fear. Eugene and Mo rushed in, and the man who'd arrived in the Lincoln labored up the stairs behind them.

"We would have brought them down," Eugene said to the man.

"Shut up, you idiot," the man said. "I'm not an invalid. I'm a Bulgarian bull."

The Bulgarian bull lunged into the room, and I thought he looked like a bull having a stroke. His face was purple, and he was sweating and breathing heavy. He was close to six-feet tall and weighed about two hundred and fifty pounds. His eyes were dilated black and glittered in his feverish face. His jowls shook when he talked. He had small, square, yellow teeth behind fleshy protruding lips. He was dressed in bagged-out

266

dark dress slacks and a white dress shirt, open at the neck, showing a mat of graying chest hair.

"So," he said, looking down at Mooner with his mean little pig eyes. "What have you got to say for yourself?"

"Dude," Mooner said.

The Bulgarian bull leaned over and got so close to Mooner their noses were touching. "Do you know who I am?" he yelled at Mooner. "I'm Gregor Bluttovich. I'm the man you cheated." And before Mooner could say anything, Bluttovich hit him open-handed on the side of the head and knocked Mooner over.

"That isn't Vinnie," I said.

Eugene and Mo sucked in air and froze.

Bluttovich turned on me. "Who's this?"

"She was with him," Eugene said. "We thought you'd like her."

"They're lying," I said. "They took the wrong man, and they were going to keep me for themselves."

Bluttovich looked over at Eugene and Mo. "Is this true?"

"She's trying to make trouble," Eugene said.

Bluttovich grunted. "I'll give her trouble." He turned away and powered himself to the door. "I'm hungry," he said. "I want something to eat, and then I'll deal with these two."

Bluttovich led the way down the stairs, and Eugene and Mo stumbled after him, closing and locking the tower door. Mooner was still stretched out on the floor, a trickle of blood oozing from a split lip.

"Are you all right?" I asked.

"He's a scary dude," Mooner said.

I went back to the window, desperate to see RangeMan in the driveway. I was counting down to the moment when Bluttovich was done eating and the real horror would begin. I was staring so intently, and wanting to see help so badly, I almost missed the movement in the woods to the right. There was no wind, but something was disturbing the undergrowth. Animal, I thought. And then more movement a few feet over. And next thing, the woods were alive with Hobbits. They were everywhere, creeping forward out of the woods onto the grass, inching up to the fortress. I ran around the room, looking out all the windows, and everywhere I looked I saw Hobbits. There were hundreds of them.

"Hobbits!" I yelled to Mooner. "Get up! There are Hobbits out there!"

Mooner got to his feet, and we looked out at the Hobbits. They were up and running now, brandishing golf clubs, baseball bats, and tennis rackets.

"Get the Orcs!" they were yelling, led by Vinnie and Chicaribbit. "Down with the evil Orcs!"

Vinnie was back in his Hobbit clothes, sprinting across the lawn, cape flying, pumping the air with his fist.

Mooner yelled at them from the tower. "Go Hobbits!"

The Hobbits looked up at Mooner and cheered. "Hobbit Ho!" they yelled, and they went into the house like Hobbit SWAT. They hurled themselves through windows and doors.

A cavalcade of black cars and one red Firebird raced up the driveway, and a chopper whirred overhead. Ranger was out of the first car. Morelli followed. They went in through the front door. Guys in FBI jackets poured out of the cars. Local police cars rolled in and parked on the grass.

I heard footsteps on the stairs leading to the tower room, and Mooner and I pressed ourselves flat against the wall, praying it wasn't going to be Bluttovich who came through the door. The door opened and Chicaribbit burst into the room. She went straight to Mooner and threw her arms around him and kissed him.

"I was so worried, Bungo Goodchild," she said.

Mooner grinned. "No problemo," he said. "And I've still got my nuts."

Ranger was next through the door, followed by twenty or thirty Hobbits, who swirled around Mooner and looked out the windows and commented on the woods and how this would make a wonderful Shire.

Ranger cut the plastic cuffs off my hands. "Are you okay?" he asked.

I nodded. "Yes. How did you find us so fast?"

"Vinnie and the Hobbits got to the parking lot just as the van was leaving with you and Mooner. Vinnie had your purse, so they were able to follow the van in the Mercedes."

"What was Vinnie doing with my purse?"

"He thought you'd have a gun in it. And you did have a gun, but turns out you had something even better. You had car keys and a cell phone."

"Vinnie called you."

"Yes. And I called Morelli, and he did his cop thing. Turned out it was easy to organize. The feds have been following Bluttovich for months."

"Who called the Hobbits?"

"The Hobbits called the Hobbits. They were uncontrollable. The fear was that they would rush the house before Bluttovich got here, and the police wouldn't be able to charge him with anything." Ranger grinned. "The truth is, the Hobbits saved the day. They caught Bluttovich by surprise and no one got hurt."

Lula and Connie came through the door.

"Heart attack," Lula said. "I'm having a heart attack. How the heck many stairs is that? Give me room. Give me air." She spotted me and grabbed me and hugged me. "Connie and me were so scared for you."

Connie joined in the hug. "It's over," she said. "They got all the Orcs."

"We were in communication with Vinnie and the Hobbits right from the beginning," Lula said. "So we know all about Orcs."

"They're the enemy of Hobbits," Connie said.

"I want to see Bluttovich," I said to Ranger.

"Babe," Ranger said.

"Who's Bluttovich?" Connie wanted to know.

"He's the bad guy," I said. "He's the one who caused all the death and destruction."

"Count me in," Lula said. "I want to see him, too."

We found Bluttovich in the kitchen. He was cuffed, along with Mo, Eugene, the driver, and the other guy who helped with my abduction. Even in cuffs,

270

Bluttovich was frightening, exuding anger like a toxic gas.

"You!" he said, fixing his crazy eyes on me.

I didn't say anything to Bluttovich. I didn't have to. I just wanted to see him in cuffs and know I was in the power seat. I felt good.

Lula was behind me. "What's with the bump on your forehead?" she asked Bluttovich. "It's big as a baseball."

Bluttovich glared at Lula and snarled.

"Cripes," Lula said to Bluttovich. "What the heck's the matter with you? Where's your manners?"

"Some guy in a cape called him an Orc and hit him with a bottle," Eugene said. "We were sitting at the table, eating sandwiches, and next thing, all these Hobbits invaded the house and this one Hobbit rushed at Gregor with a red beer bottle and hit him in the head. And then the Hobbit kissed the bottle, and said it was his precious. If I didn't know better, I'd swear the Hobbit looked like Vincent Plum."

Morelli was on the other side of the room, talking to three guys in FBI jackets. They all had pads out, taking notes. Morelli was talking to the FBI guys, but he was looking at me. Our eyes caught and held for a moment, and he smiled.

I left the gray stone fortress with Lula, Connie, and Vinnie.

"You hit Bluttovich with my lucky bottle, didn't you?" I said to Vinnie when Lula turned onto River Road.

"Yeah," Vinnie said. "It was beautiful. We caught them all flat-footed. I saw Bluttovich at the table, and it all came together for me. I saw him at Sunflower's house the day it burned down. I could have shot him. I had your gun, but I knew the cops were right behind us, so I smacked him in the face with the bottle."

"So it was a lucky bottle after all," Lula said.

"It's not a lucky bottle," Vinnie said. "It's Lucky's bottle. I talked to my mom this morning, and she said it was no secret about the bottle. Lucky was Pip's guinea pig. Lucky's ashes are in the bottle. Pip left it to Stephanie because she has a hamster. I guess he figured there was a rodent connection."

I turned and stared at Vinnie. "All this time I've been carrying guinea pig ashes around?"

"Yeah," Vinnie said. "Isn't that a kicker?"

"I don't mean to change the subject," Lula said. "But we don't got no bonds agency. What are we supposed to do every day?"

"And I don't have Lucille," Vinnie said.

"I bet I could help with that," Lula said. "Maureen Brown and me are still friends. Suppose I get her to talk to Harry and tell him how it was all a misunderstanding and she wasn't actually doing the dirty with you. Like, we could say her brother needed bonding out, and you were advising her."

"Do you think Harry will believe that?" Vinnie asked.

"As a student of human nature, I learned that people believe what they want to believe," Lula said. "Anyways, if we can get you and Lucille together, and Harry don't want to kill you no more, maybe we can get him back into the bail bonds business. And if that happens, I want a couch that vibrates."

"You got it," Vinnie said.

Connie's car was parked at the demolished bonds office. Lula dropped her first. Vinnie and I were next. Lula dropped us in my parking lot. Mooner and Chicaribbit and a bunch more Hobbits were right behind us in my Mercedes.

"Hey, dudes," Mooner said to Vinnie and me. "Party tonight in the Love Bus."

We both passed, and Mooner transferred the Hobbits to the RV and drove off.

"If I could borrow the Mercedes, I'd go try to talk to Lucille," Vinnie said. "Maybe she's calmed down. Maybe she misses me, too."

I gave him the key. "Good luck."

I let myself into my apartment and listened to the quiet. No Hobbits. No Vinnie. Just Rex and the soft whir of his wheel going round. I took Lucky's bottle out of my purse and set it on the counter, next to Rex's cage. I made a peanut butter sandwich and washed it down with my last beer.

I was still in the kitchen when Ranger called.

"Just checking in to make sure you're at home and safe," he said.

"I'm fine," I told him. "How about you?"

"I'm good. We went through Bluttovich's house and found enough drugs and stolen property to put him away for a long time. And the feds confiscated his files and computer. I'm sure they'll find more evidence against him. And his crew will talk. Those guys aren't heroes, and they don't like Bluttovich. I'm going out of the country for a few weeks. Tank will watch out for you. And I'll be on my cell phone. I'll be in touch when I get back. You owe me." And he disconnected.

I took a shower and was about to dry my hair when my doorbell buzzed. I wrapped myself in a bath towel, went to the door, and looked out the security peephole at Morelli.

"What?" I asked, holding the door partially open.

"Can I come in?"

"I'm not dressed."

Morelli stepped into my apartment and closed and locked the door behind him. "That's perfect," he said, "because I have something for you to wear." And he dangled a lacy pink thong from his finger. "I stopped at the mall on the way home just now. I thought you'd look pretty in this."